BUNCH QUITTER

He'd fought to stay alive for six months . . .

And when he returned to his home town, Chance Ragan had just one thing in mind—to prove he was as good a cowhand as he'd ever been—and that was the best.

But he found he'd run smack into the roughest deal he'd ever tackled. Before he was done, he'd fought his way with hands and teeth and feet through three of the town's toughest bullies—and even then he still had to prove he was as fast with a gun as he'd always been.

BUNCH QUITTER

Chad Merriman

GUNSMOKE

First published in the UK by Panther Books

This hardback edition 2008
by BBC Audiobooks Ltd
by arrangement with
Golden West Literary Agency

ISBN 978 1 405 68193 3

British Library Cataloguing in Publication Data available.

Printed and bound in Great Britain by
Antony Rowe Ltd., Chippenham, Wiltshire

1

IT COULD be mighty hard to knock on a door. Ragan figured he would rather take a licking than put his knuckles on the panel at his back. His thin, long hand on the railing trembled; he could feel the throbbing of the steamboat come up from the engines through the wood of the hull.

The shaking he detested was his own entirely. He knew that. He had the jitters. But there wasn't much time left to ask Kildane for his old job back. They would land at Dalles City in a few minutes. Afterward it would be even harder to approach the man. Ragan swore at himself, silently and in impotent anger.

He was a cowpoke, wasted to weakness by the long hospital months, and this river was the way back to the range. They called it the Columbia, a desert river long before it came into valley greenery. He yearned to be home. He wanted to feel leather on the flats of his thighs again, the wind sweet with heat and sage on his face. He wanted rimrock, the yellow, rough country of the John Day river, a sky deeper than any other on earth. He was done with cities and congestion, above all he was sick of idleness.

The steamboat's steady wheeling had shoved her upstream from Crate's Point. The river had bent south, now, and where shortly it swung back again lay the town where he would get off. So would Judd Kildane. Much simpler, Ragan thought in his mental paralysis, to brace him for a job now—before he went ashore. Kildane had plenty of money. He would put up at the Umatilla House while, this time, Chance Ragan would sleep in the cheapest hotel in town. They wouldn't meet, probably. They would no longer move in the same circle.

Heat broke sharp and yellow on the desert ahead. There had been fogs in the gorge of the Cascades, during the day's long run, thick-layered, depressing, heavy. Glancing upstream, where the bare basalt turned soft with heat, Ragan had a sudden lift of spirit.

5

The eastern and western sections of Oregon changed that quickly in nature. Green hills and valleys turned sharply into sageland wastes. Into the cow country, the grassy ranges—into home. Maybe he could change as swiftly, now that he was so nearly back again. Hadn't he been altered overnight, involuntarily, last winter in that blizzard? He sure had. From a strapping man of action into an idle cripple afraid to ask for a riding job because he looked unfit for such rough work.

Sound stirred Ragan out of his long, lost thoughts. The door of the cabin behind had opened, its hinges creaking a little. But it hadn't been Kildane's door, for a wavering female voice spoke behind him.

"We coming into Dalles City?"

Turning, he saw a very old woman in the doorway of the cabin next to Kildane's. Her thin white hair was in disarray, her eyes puffed and bloodshot. She steadied herself by a hand on the door jamb, but her swaying was much greater than that of the packet.

She's drunker'n a lord, Ragan thought.

He touched his hat. "Yes, ma'am. That where you're getting off?"

"Yes. Not that it matters much. One place is like another." She shrugged her shoulders. They sloped sharply and looked very tired. They were a good deal like his own. He was suddenly and ineffably concerned about her. He could smell the gin, heavy and offensive, on her breath as he stepped closer—In that way they were different. He liked whiskey.

"You got friends there, ma'am?" he asked, wondering what would become of this old drunk in so tough a town.

"I haven't any friends."

Ragan said, in dawning recognition, "Would you be Poker Annie?"

"What's left of her. What made you think so?"

"Why—why I reckon you're still a pretty famous woman, ma'am."

She laughed without mirth. "A famous old she-soak."

He felt awkward and wished he'd kept his mouth shut. What this woman had left of fame was really notoriety, as she implied. Once she had been the toast of the California placer fields, a fabulous, beautiful woman gambler. Twenty years ago, that was. He had heard of her drifting now, the fortune she had made wasted away with the beauty. A wanderer, destroyed by what?

6

She frightened him and touched in him in some deep nerve of sympathy.

He said, "My old man used to go to your place in Sacramento. I remember him saying he'd never seen a more beautiful woman."

She looked at him wonderingly. Her face changed, softening and losing a little of its waste. She seemed to feel better, just remembering with him. She seemed to like him all at once, and this was a good feeling to Ragan.

"Did I know your father?"

He laughed. "He never had any gold dust to risk at your table, ma'am. Said he only went there to look at you."

"Thanks, and luck to you. Not many bother to cheer up an old woman." She moved back into the cabin and closed the door. Maybe to be alone with the memory he had freshened in her. Ragan was glad he'd been able to do it. He was glad she hadn't known what kind of man he had been before waste had been inflicted upon him, too.

Angrily he swung about and took the three steps to the Kildane door, trying from habit to conceal his limp. Then he quit trying to hide it and was a little more coldly furious when his knuckles rapped briskly on the wood.

If Judd don't want me again, he told himself, the hell with him. Somehow, in talking with Poker Annie, he had put his bad moment behind him.

The drumming brought a deep, drowsy call from inside the cabin. The voice was a man's—Kildane's.

"Who's that?"

Ragan didn't answer. The son-of-a-bitch can come and see, he thought. They said I'd die, and I didn't. They'll think I'm no good any more but, by God, I'll show 'em. Nothing this side of hell can beat me into a drunken tramp like Annie.

Yet it nearly buckled his knees when the door swung open to disclose a girl. So long remembered, so dark and slim and supple. His breath caught and the sweetness he had known with her rolled through him. But not for long. Sweetness had gone out of his life, with so many other things, last winter.

"Joy," he said.

"Why, Chance—hello."

Beyond her Ragan saw a man shove to a sit on the cabin bunk. He had been the one who called out. Now he looked at Ragan with a sharp, probing interest. There was shock on his face that sagged his mouth and stretched the length of

7

his eyes. Few who had known the old Ragan could conceal that surprise the way Joy had, just now.

"Come in, Chance," Joy said when her brother failed to offer the invitation.

Ragan's hand went up to his battered hat and brought it off. He had dreaded her seeing him for the first time since the trouble, and now it was over. Again he remembered not to hide his limp when he stepped on inside the cabin. He didn't care that he was gaunt, shabby and busted. He didn't give a damn, suddenly, whether Judd had a job to offer. He had never truckled to any man and never would.

Judd had lifted himself off the bunk. He smiled, finally, holding out his hand. It was a long, lean hand attached to a long, lean body. His hair and eyes were the color of Joy's, but the eyes lacked the present warmth of hers. Judd's never had held much depth.

"So you're going back." Judd offered. Then, because it was in him to sink a barb where he could, he added, "To stay?"

Ragan stared at him, blunt and hard and almost indifferent. "Depends on whether I can find a riding job, Judd."

The question that comment implied hung an awkwardness in the air. The Kildanes' Teeter was the largest outfit on the John Day. If anybody in that country could use an extra rider, it would be Kildane. Ragan had spoken his piece. He let it ride and waited.

Joy had seated herself on the edge of the bunk to make room for the standing men. Watching her covertly, Ragan saw a plea form on her exquisite face as she looked up at her brother. The eyes were brown, and the plea changed to command. Ragan didn't like that. He wanted Judd to decide whether there was a job for him on Teeter. A year ago the man would have been glad to have him back on his payroll. But a year was a long, long time. It could turn white to black, sweet to bitter, friends to wary strangers.

With a wry smile, Judd said, "Your prospects aren't very good, Chance. I've laid off hands, myself. Won't Terrebine take you back into the business with him?" His voice implied that this would be a charity on the part of Terrebine.

Ragan squared his shoulders, but they still were boney under his coat. "You didn't hear? It takes money to pay hospital bills like I piled up. I had to sell him my half of the cattle company."

"I guess he did mention it," Judd admitted. He had nothing further to offer.

The awkwardness that still filled the cabin put a flush on Joy's brown cheeks. She tossed her head and made a strained smile for Ragan. The mouth was flared-lipped, lovely, but now its expression was shallow.

"I wish you'd got in touch sooner, Chance," she said. "It's been a monotonous day with nobody but Judd to talk to. But maybe you'll be on the Canyon City stage, tomorrow."

"Likely buy me a horse," Ragan said vaguely, although he didn't have anything like the necessary money. He just didn't want to see either one of them tomorrow.

He turned and went out. That was the only move that Chance had left.

Joy hurried after him, carefully closing the door behind her. She called softly, "Chance, wait a minute."

He stopped with his back to the rail, facing her, his eyes withdrawn, his features unmoving. They both knew how baldly Judd had lied about laying off men. There was a beef boom throughout the country because of the mining activity. Teeter was plenty busy.

Coming up to him, she almost whispered, "Why didn't you answer my letter?"

"I don't know."

"I wrote as soon as I heard they'd taken you to the hospital. When you didn't answer—well, I assumed the obvious."

"There was a question," he said harshly, "as to whether I'd ever be back here. When that was answered, there was one of whether there was any use in me coming home."

"Oh, there is."

"That's not proven."

She was bewildered by his glinting anger and, all at once, passive and constrained.

"What's the matter, Chance?" she asked finally. "What's so wrong?"

"Judd just showed you what was wrong. And the hell with him."

"And me, too?" The erect shoulders pulled straighter with that question.

"With anybody who figures I'm no damned good any more."

"Such a thought never entered my mind."

"Maybe it's just not settled there, like it is in Judd's mind."

Her eyes searched him. She seemed about to say more.

9

Then he saw the impulse die. She turned back toward the cabin door, angry and not wanting to be. He went the other way, along the side deck toward the open space ahead of the cabins.

Dalles City sprawled and brawled at the foot of a great brown hill, at the edge of the river. Not only was it the capital of the great Oregon cattle ranges—presently it was also a trans-shipping point for freight moving to the Blue Mountain and Bitterroot mines; a fleshpot for the punchers and miners passing through. It was a teeming, raw, sunscorched desert town of rock and sage and pine and gleaming water.

The *Queen* slid in against the wharf-boat and made fast her lines. When her gangplank fell ashore, Ragan went down with the first rush. Most of the passengers would stop overnight before taking the portage train to the Deschutes Landing. There, above the long rapids, another packet could be taken for the towns up-river.

But the John Day Valley lay beyond two hundred miles of sky and desert. A man could take a Concord stage, walk it or fork leather. Not only did Ragan lack the money to buy the saddler he had mentioned to Joy. He lacked stage fare. He lacked the strength, at present, to walk two hundred miles. But he was going to get there and make a living again, and to hell with the man or woman who doubted that he could do it.

Tramping along Front Street in his careful stride, he observed that the trees were dropping leaves. That was the only sign of autumn in all the hot sunlight. When he reached Court Street, he halted. Then, making up his mind, he went on along Front. From here on his would be the shabbier part of a town.

There was activity all down the wheeled-up length of the thoroughfare. Saddle horses at the hitch bars outnumbered the wagon teams slumped at intervals. The stage rolled in from Umatilla way and wheeled up before the express office. Ragan saw few punchers. There were more red-shirted miners and red-blanketed Indians.

But a man came hurrying along the walk toward him, shouldering through the crowd. He wore Levis, scuffed boots and a highcrowned hat. His gun and spurs evoked familiar memories in Ragan, sharpening his longing.

The man looked up and nearly let his glance slide past

10

Ragan. Then his eyes widened in recognition. His brown face broke into a smile.

"Chance! You orey-eyed old buckaroo!" he yelled.

"Howdy, Pace," Chance Ragan said and for the first time in months felt alive. His grin rode deep and easy on his face.

"Why didn't you let a man know you were heading back this way?" Hanna was a stocky man whose black hair was grey around the ears. He didn't wait for an answer—he grabbed Ragan's hand and held onto it. "Chance, you son-of-a-gun, I've got an appointment with the Land Commissioner, and I'm late already. I've got a room at the Bradford. You go there and wait for me, and we'll sure drink on it."

"Sure," Ragan said. Somebody was glad to see him back. Really glad. Glad all over. That did more for him than half a dozen slugs of whiskey.

Hanna let go his hand and rushed on. The warmth remained in Ragan's face as he tramped on in his irregular stride. He was almost, but not quite, back in God's country.

The Bradford Hotel was on up Front. It was a less pretentious place then the Umatilla House, where Judd and Joy Kildane would wait for the next day's stage to Canyon City. Ragan had the price of a room and decided to register at the Bradford and wait for Pace to get back. With Pace Hanna it didn't matter where the hell you were.

He owed a lot to Pace, who had saved him from the blizzard. Except for the man's quick, knowing care—the doctor had told Ragan later—he would have lost a leg and maybe a hand or, more probably, would have died and been done with it all. Pace didn't know that yet, and anyway would be impatient with any show of gratitude.

Ragan signed for a room, accepted a key and mounted the hotel stairs. He let himself into a small hot space and dropped his roll on the bed. He tossed his hat after the gear, then peeled off the coat of his cheap dark suit. Unlike Portland, which was beginning to be a city, this was a shirt-sleeves town. He was getting back into harness.

He yawned, easing and feeling more and more that he was where he belongd. Soon the rest would be there, the bulge of leather beneath him, the stitching of horse's hoofs, the yellow seas of bunchgrass. These things would erase from his mind the sickening swirl of snowflakes, the bite of killing wind, the months when he had fought to keep them from taking off a gangrenous leg and arm. Appendages left weak-

11

ened and clumsy, where he had been a man of extraordinary agility before.

That was what hurt really, as it must hurt Poker Annie—the way he had stood out before.

He was napping when Hanna walked in, unbidden. Pace carried a bottle of whiskey under his arm and had an extra water glass in his hand. He put these on the stand table and pushed back his hat. Again his casual, friendly smile did what the bottle was supposed to do. Ragan grinned back, and it came quick and easy.

"I hoped you'd register, so I looked," Pace said. "Chance, here I'm bringing a drink to the man I said I'd beat the hell out of, the first time I seen him. Nancy wrote you a passle of letters while you was in the hospital. You ignored every damned one. No man can do that to my daughter and not get a hiding."

Angrily, Ragan held up his hands.

"About that time I couldn't hold a pencil, let alone write."

But the fingers didn't show much of that weakness now. The countless times he had squeezed a rubber ball had restored their flexibility and some of his control of them. He could draw and fire a sixgun with much of his old speed and accuracy.

God knew he had done that, drawing over and over, in a cheap room in Portland, after he'd become an out-patient. Each time he practiced he'd seen the featureless face of the man who had set him afoot in the Blue Mountains, in that blizzard, and cost him so much of time and pain and pride.

"They got nurses," Pace grunted, pouring whiskey, "that'll do a man's writin' for him."

"They got nobody," Ragan barked, "to tell him if a girl'd care to hear from a bugger with only one leg and hand."

"It come that close, did it?" Pace said mildly.

"They said I couldn't keep 'em and live," Ragan returned. "But I kept 'em and lived. Until I did, I figured no girl ought to be thinking about me."

"Here. You need it." Pace handed Ragan a glass nearly full of whiskey.

Ragan's thin fingers wrapped around the heavy glass—his bad ones, just to prove once more that he could do it. The weak arm lifted the whiskey to his lips. It brought the glass down empty.

"Not so goddam fast," Pace said. "Me, I ain't a camel. I figured that'd last through a few questions."

"Such as?"

"First, who shot your horse from under you?"

"I just don't know."

"But you think you know."

"Mebbe," Ragan admitted.

Pace filled the glass again. "All right. If you ain't talkin', then drink. You ain't sure who did it, but you aim to find out and kill him. That's why you come back."

Ragan shook his head. "Not entirely. Mainly, I got to eat. To eat, I got to work. It's that simple. And that tough. Judd Kildane was on the steamboat and turned me down cold. Like the rest will. I don't blame 'em. The way it looks, there ain't a day's work left in me worth paying for. But, by God, that's wrong."

"You got a bum slant," Pace said, "on how you look to people. What's happening is you see yourself through your own eyes, all the time. Comparin' what's now with what used to be. That's no good. Nothin' lasts forever."

"The answer it gives is close enough."

"It could be a mile off," Pace snapped. "Nobody knows what you wish you was, instead of are. And nobody's all he'd like to be, even when nothing's happened to him. I sure as hell ain't. Not by a damsite."

"I used to like what I was well enough."

"Which is why you can't take a change."

"I don't aim to take it," Ragan said fiercely. "Let's get off that subject, Pace. Tell me what's doing on the John Day."

Pace seated himself on the bed, took a pull on his drink, and said, "Not much is different. There's still a mining boom, and the cowmen'll have a beef boom as long as that's so. Arch Terrebine's still buying most of the valley market cut. Except mine and Kitch Dunsan's. We just won't sell to that man."

In mild surprise, Ragan said, "Howcome? When I done the buying for the company you sold to me quick enough."

"You ain't Terrebine, even if you once was his pardner."

"Who's doing his buying now?"

"Angel Younts," Pace said with a grimace. "But he's only one reason I won't do business with the new Terrebine Cattle Company. Me and Kitch figure to sell to the Wyoming drivers at Baker City. More work and less money, but we'll like it better."

"I got anything to do with that attitude?"

13

"You sure have." Pace had emptied his own glass. He cupped it in his hand and leaned forward. "To start with, it was a rotten thing for Terrebine to buy you out when you needed money. The company's rolling in it now. He could have carried you along, and a right man would have done that for his pardner."

"He jumped at the chance to get things in his own hands. But I didn't have any choice."

"You hear anything about his doings after he bought you out?"

Ragan shook his head. "Only what Nancy wrote me. That the man's now singing loud. Got his own butcher shops in the mining camps, even."

"Auburn, Canyon City, Baker, Eldorado. And all the other big ones. Where he couldn't talk a butcher into selling out to him, he opened a new shop and run the cuss outta business. When he had the only shops in camp, the price of beef hit the ceiling. But not the price to the cowmen. They get no more now than they ever did, and I think less."

"That don't surprise me."

"But it was something he couldn't have pulled off with you his pardner."

Reaching for the bottle, Ragan tipped more whiskey into his glass. His hand shook as he threw the liquor against the back of his mouth and let it wash down his throat.

He said, "You're trying to tell me something you don't want to say right out."

"I'll say it right out," Pace returned. "Whoever shot your horse, that night in a blizzard, set things up real nice for Terrebine."

"Which means he shot the cayuse or had somebody else do it."

"Which means just that."

"How fast did he expand, afterward?" Ragan asked.

"All at once. Mushroomed to hell and gone."

"Where'd he get the money? The company never had that kind of dinero in my day."

"Somebody's backing him."

"When I find out who, I got two men to kill," Ragan reflected.

"When you know for sure," Pace agreed, "you have."

"I'll know for sure, and I'll do it."

Hanna got up from his chair to leave, wedgy and quick-moving. Ragan rose more slowly, and when he had come to

14

a full stand he towered some four inches over Hanna. He was heavy-framed, big-boned, built to carry far more flesh than he now did. His square jaw, because of the thinness, gave his face a strong stubbornness. The slowness of his motions, now, nettled him.

He had been made for action, incisive and often sudden. Those instincts remained in him undiminished, so that time after time he must be reminded of his handicaps—and his hatred of those responsible for them.

2

RAGAN STARED at the door a long while after Hanna had left. Pace had only confirmed suspicions that had nagged at his own mind all along. Slowly Ragan's sharp face lost the geniality engendered by the man's visit. Again he relived that evening when the trouble had come to him, high in the Blue Mountains.

He had been riding across the range from Auburn, where he had delivered a cut of steers to the local butcher. He had climbed into a heavy fall of snow. As he descended into the valley he had found even worse weather. Still short of Susanville, his destination, a rifle shot from a closeby rim-rock had dropped his horse. There had been no warning, nothing in preceding events to prompt him to caution.

It was primitive country, inhabited only by a few moon-shiners who made rotgut for the miners. For a while he believed that he had been mistaken for somebody else. He had left the dead horse and proceeded afoot, the closest place he could head for being Hanna's little Ladder outfit on Wildcat Creek. Long before he got there, floundering through the snow afoot, the white storm-curtain had wiped out all landmarks.

Hanna had stumbled onto him the next morning, two miles short of Ladder headquarters, unconscious and nearly dead. Ragan had only a feverish, disjointed memory of the rest. He must have kept going until the storm was nearly over. Hanna, taking a look at his steers, afterward, had found him there in the drift.

Pace had rushed him by sleigh to Susanville, where the doctor sent him on to Dalles City. At the river town, another medico had placed him on a steamboat and hurried him down to Portland and one of its hospitals. The worst had come after that.

Ragan's skin turned clammy when he remembered the weeks in which he fought the doctors to a standstill. They had claimed that his right leg and arm, frostbitten and now gangrenous, had to come off to save his life. He had sworn to kill the man who touched him with a knife.

And from somewhere his will had drawn healing power, not complete, not perfect, but enough that he still had an arm and leg on his right side. And a hate inside him. He was sure now that somebody had waylaid and left him for dead. Since then Arch Terrebine had prospered in a way that would have been impossible under the old partnership.

This bitter remembering was broken by a knock on the door. When Ragan opened up, a boy stood there.

"You Chance Ragan?" the lad asked. "The lady said I was to keep lookin' till I found you."

Ragan accepted the envelope the boy held out to him. He fished into his pocket, found two-bits and handed the coin to the lad. Stepping back into the room, he closed the door and found that he was trembling. The stationery was that of the Umatilla House. His name was written across the face of the envelope in the hand of a woman.

Joy Kildane.

He tore the letter open and pulled out the note within. The message was brief: *The inevitable has happened. Judd met friends and has deserted me for the evening. Why don't you come over for that visit we missed on the steamboat?*

There was no signature, nor did there need to be one. Ragan looked down at his rumpled suit, and his raised spirits deserted him. He dropped the note onto the table. Then the defiance that had come to him at the door of Kildane's cabin rose up to dislodge that weakness. To hell with uncertainty and hesitation. He got into his coat and pulled on his hat.

He descended the stairway of the hotel, crossed a lamp-lighted lobby and came out onto the street. There was no use denying his desire to see Joy again—and alone. Theirs had been an odd relationship. As mistress of Teeter, she had seemed out of his reach, back in the days when he had held down a puncher's job on the spread. Later, when he

16

and Terrebine had started supplying beef to the mining camps, he'd had more of a break with her.

She had been friendlier, impressed by his enterprise and mounting success. Even then he had not been able to see her regularly, his work taking him to all parts of the Oregon desert to buy cattle. Yet, before the big trouble, he had begun to detect in her a response to the hungers growing within himself.

He paced the length of the sidewalk, crossed the street, and from the next corner could see the Umatilla House, bright with light at the river's edge. He headed for the place, again not caring that he limped, that he was shabby, broke, and what some would say was licked already.

Her room proved to be on the second floor, and she welcomed him warmly.

"I didn't know what luck the boy would have finding you," she said. "I'm glad you came."

She shut the door, enclosing them in their first real privacy in a long while. She looked at him, smiling. Almost, he thought, he could have taken her in his arms then and had the welcome he wanted. He was glad she had not taken real offense at his temper, there on the packet. His good humor had been somewhat restored.

She said, "Sit down, Chance, and tell me all about it."

"Beginning where?" he asked, taking a seat, not caring that he dropped into it clumsily.

"Do you have any idea who tried to kill you?"

"A good answer to that question," Ragan said, "is to ask another. Who profited the most from what happened to me?"

He saw shock enter her face as she stared at him sharply. "Are you alluding to Arch Terrebine?"

"Does he answer the question?"

"Why, I guess. In a way. But that's preposterous."

"Is it?" asked Ragan. "But there could be other answers. I hear Angel Younts come into the company after I sold my interest. Buying steers in my place—which is something he couldn't have done with me around."

She gave his eyes a thoughtful study. "You're awfully bitter, aren't you? Younts, maybe. But Arch isn't a man who'd try to murder you. I know that."

"Been seeing a lot of him?"

She flushed. "No more than I've seen of other men. Chance, you offended me deeply. I wrote you a letter as soon

17

as I heard about your trouble. When you didn't answer it, what did you expect me to think?"

"You're right. I've got no kick coming there."

"And you're going to regain the ground you lost," she said fiercely. "I know wou will. It doesn't have to be in the cattle business. There are other opportunities just as promising. Why don't you prospect, Chance? I can't think of a way for a man to get back on his feet any quicker."

Ragan grinned. "If he has luck. Which four out of five don't have. Lately mine's run sour."

"You better get back in the habit of trusting your luck," she insisted.

"Joy, I got a feeling that man's success means a lot to you."

"Why not? It's a man's business to be successful. You're all measured by that standard."

"And what's the measure of a woman?" he asked.

"Her ability to love and help."

"Which comes easier when a man's a success."

Again temper made its hint in her eyes. "What's the matter with you? You didn't used to be so cynical."

"It's the first time I was set back to taw," he retorted, "and had to figure things out again."

"I was only trying to help you."

With what? he wondered. His building himself back into what she could call success? The Kildanes had money and pride of place. He knew that. It had once been the barrier he felt between them; he felt it again. She seemed to have grown aware of it anew, was already tackling it, trying to tear it down. That took the edge off his pleasure in being with her. He should see that obstacle; she should not.

Boots came along the hallway. There was a muffled knock on the door, then it opened without Joy's bidding. But she seemed to have recognized the knock, and Judd Kildane came through. His face settled into a look of surprise. He flung his sister a glance of brittle wonder.

But Ragan saw that less than the flush on Joy's cheeks, an expression that was almost guilty. Then she made the barest toss of her head. By then Ragan knew what neither Kildane had been actor enough to conceal, that Judd was angered by this situation, probably had forbidden its taking place.

Recovering, Judd said, "Howdy again, Chance. Joy, I come up to tell you Sara Lansing's in town. I seen Dave. I figured

18

you two women could pass the time together. Dave and some more of us want to poker a little."

"A safer pastime for her than this?" Ragan said softly.

Judd flung him a look of quick temper. "How did I know you two would get together?"

"Afraid of it, though, weren't you?"

"Why the chip on your shoulder, Chance?" Judd demanded. "You sore because I said Teeter don't have a job for you, right now? It just don't, that's all. I know you better than try to make a place for you. You'd catch on and be sorer yet. Come on down to the bar, and let's have a drink."

Ragan nodded, aware that Judd was only trying to horn him out of Joy's room. Once Chance Ragan had been good enough to visit with his sister. Not now—not until and unless he got back his place as one of the valley's successful men. He had strongly sensed the same attitude in Joy. But he felt that she was happy to have him back on the John Day. He was less sure that Judd wanted him anywhere in the country.

Terrebine again, Ragan thought. Judd always tried to shoo her toward him . . .

He picked up his hat, nodded to a puzzled, half-angry Joy, and followed Judd out. But at the foot of the stairs, he said, "We'll postpone that drink a while. I've had enough for one night."

"Later, then," Judd said. He was not quite able to conceal his relief.

Am I jumping to the wrong conclusions, Ragan wondered as he walked on alone, or am I beginning to see things straight for the first time?

He was halfway back to the hotel when he saw Poker Annie again, weaving along the sidewalk. Transients rushing to the gold fields or out again jostled her impatiently. None of them knew Annie had witnessed a gold rush that made this one, big as it was, look piddling. Ragan had another angry sympathy for her, dislodged and discarded as she was, so nearly like himself.

He touched his hat as he stopped before her. She made as if to go around, wearily, not recognizing him immediately, seeing only one more obstacle. The apathy and utter futility of that made Ragan speak to her.

"Howdy again, Annie. Don't you have a hotel room? These streets get crowded and rough this time of night."

The vague eyes peered at him. "It's the nice man from the

steamboat. I've got a room. I didn't like it. I hate my own company. Would you like a drink with an old tosspot?"

"Why not?" said Ragan. "I'm just sort of a young one."

A little later, when he was in Annie's cheap hotel room, nursing whiskey, he wondered what Judd would think after the drink he had turned down in the sumptuous bar of the Umatilla House. But this was more to Ragan's liking, this kind of company. Anne had a sort of dignity about her as she played hostess, lingering instinctively from the days when she had been the gold field's belle. In the pale yellow lamplight, she was a strange echo to her young and pretty years.

He tipped his glass to hers and said, "To the old days, ma'am."

She shook her head. "They're gone, and everything that was any good with them. Son, why do you bother with an old stew like me?"

"In the first place, it's no bother. Then I'm curious. Would you want it to happen again? I mean having a lot, then losing it?"

Her face changed, softening. Suddenly a clawlike hand came out and rested on his arm. Its touch was gentle.

"I have a notion you've been hurt."

"It's not that—" he began.

But her eyes turned vague, and she didn't seem to hear him because of her thinking. Then, "The cases aren't the same. What I lost, time took from me, the same as it does from everybody. And that don't come into what *you* lost or think you did. With you, time'll help."

"It won't grow me a good leg and arm."

"It'll grow almost anything you plant in it. I ought to know." Suddenly Annie smiled. "You go now. I like my room better. I think I can sleep."

Ragan had a feeling that he could, also.

3

Chance Ragan arrived in Canyon City on the bullplank of Barney Callahan's freight outfit. Six days of burning sun, of limitless plateaus and roaring gorges had brought him home to the great, fertile valley of the John Day river. He was worn out but still going.

For endless hours he had worked Callahan's brake, heard his cussing and taken his amiable abuse. He had roused from drugged sleep, at nights, to move picket pins. He had spanned up the teams in the morning and unhooked them in late afternoon. His sweat had runnelled the dust that coated his skin, yet he had begun to feel useful, capable, better than he had in months.

At the Canyon City wagonyard, Callahan said, "You more than earned your ride, Ragan. Come on. I'll buy the drinks."

"Sure," said Ragan.

He caught up his roll and tramped out with the teamster to the street. The camp stood on the bank of Canyon Creek, in the narrows of its gorge. Miners, pack mules and buckaroos' cow ponies cluttered the long single street.

Ragan drank with Callahan in Steamboat Smith's saloon, declined an invitation to make a night of it and prepared to leave for the country farther north.

"Figure I still owe you something," Callahan said worriedly. "You sure worked." He was Irish, freckled and burned red by desert sun. His squinted eyes spoke a liking for Ragan.

"I got here," said Ragan. "That's all I wanted from it."

They shook hands, and he left, the whiskey warming him. He sniffed the air and felt excitement rise, and with it the resolve that had brought him home. He was going back to Cottonwood, up in the heart of the valley, and now he gave thought to getting there.

There might be a Cottonwood horse at one of the feed corrals. It was the custom of the country's stablemen to exchange mounts back and forth, according to travelers' needs. If someone had come in from Cottonwood and left a horse for somebody else to return later, Ragan could ride it home. Once more he'd be pounding leather.

He had just enough money left to keep him for a few days while he looked for a job. A man had to eat, no matter what else drove him. To eat, a Chance Ragan needed a horse and rope and chore, so he could do his natural work and earn his pay. Somewhere his place was waiting.

He was moving north down the canyon when a friendly, feminine voice called, "Hello, Chance. You got here.'

Ragan hauled around. A second later he had pulled his thin shoulders high and stiff. Joy Kildane sat in a roundback chair on the shadowy, inset porch of the Canyon Hotel. Men were in the chairs on either side of her. Because of them, Ragan for the moment forgot the girl.

Neither Arch Terrebine nor Angel Younts had changed a whit in the months that had passed, except for something new that showed in the eyes that watched him. It was wariness, Ragan thought. Ragan hadn't expected this encounter, wasn't prepared for it.

Terrebine came to his feet abruptly, a dark, long-legged man whose powerful shoulders were covered by a red shirt. He was handsome, he was smooth. And the pleasure he showed at Ragan's arrival was wholly false.

"Howdy, Chance," said Terrebine. "Joy mentioned seeing you in Dalles City. You look fine, man. Welcome home."

Ragan swung up the one step of the porch. He took the offered hand, felt its powerful grip, and let go promptly. He shuttled his glance to Angel Younts, who had tipped a nod but kept his seat. Younts was a stocky man of no complexion save for the deep weathering of his skin, for he was completely hairless, lacking even beard and eyebrows. The shining of his temples and crown suggested a halo when light was on them. Because this fit him to ironic perfection, he had been given his nickname.

Ragan said, "Thought you'd be home on Teeter by this time, Joy."

"Been there and back," she said. "Judd had business over at the courthouse."

"And," added Terrebine with no excuse, "the lady's been trying on the ring I'm having made for her here. I'm so dog-bitten proud, I've got to tell you, Chance."

Ragan's eyes were back on Joy, watching the flush that had slid into her cheeks. But Terrebine hadn't yet put the ring on her finger for keeps. Her gloveless hand was bare. Ragan smiled at her. It was a ghostly expression that was the dead memory of evenings under the stars when he had been as muscular as Terrebine, as handsome, as prosperous.

He had an odd, flashing insight that told him something. If, in her Dalles City hotel room, he had promised to become a big man again, she might have postponed this thing a while. But he had given no promise. So she had come home and made her decision.

Ragan said, "Congratulations, Arch. You've been lucky. So far."

"So far," Terrebine agreed, and he watched Ragan covertly. Younts' lashless eyes stared unblinkingly at Ragan, also.

Ragan touched a finger to his hatbrim, said, "So long," to Joy and left them. He guessed she had wanted him to learn promptly of her decision. Otherwise she would not have invited that meeting. It didn't matter, probably. He had lost a lot, so much that a little more ought not to make much difference.

There had been no doubt that Terrebine had wanted their position made clear. Where once they had been partners, they were now potential enemies. One day, it was a dead certainty, they would face each other over guns. Ragan knew that in the depths of his mind. There was one man he meant to kill. Angel Younts or someone else was another.

He rode on for Cottonwood through the rest of that day, following the Pendleton trail. The valley widened, and pine stood on the low mountains in a blaze of golden sun.

In late afternoon he came down from the bluff of Porcupine Creek and crossed a wooden bridge. Cottonwood lay before him, a raw and violent town. The old trees of the creek bottom shaded its rough houses and its false-fronted business street.

Roads and trails ran out of the town to the hill ranches along the upper north branch of the river and into the habitable parts of the middle fork. All about, now, were the placer camps that had sprung up in the mining boom. Yet Cottonwood was a cowtown and would always be one. The John Day was cow country, and so in most part it was bound to remain.

Ragan pulled down on the main street an took a long, savoring look. When he had left his gear on the porch of the Roundup Hotel, he turned the hire horse over to the stableman. He was of two minds as he walked back along the planks edging the street, wondering whether to ride the grubline looking for work with some hill outfit, or if he should wait here and catch the different ranchers as they came to town.

He returned to the hotel and registered, the decision put off. He climbed the stairs to the room assigned to him and found all at once that he was tired out. The saddle had felt good to him all the way but, like whiskey, its toll came later.

Depression settled on him, for he knew it would be a long while before he could turn out the day's work a rancher expected when he paid wages. Ragan lay back on the bed.

Thoughts began to stream through his mind because he had lain this way and thought one ceaseless thought too long. But there was something new in his mind now: what Hanna had told him about Terrebine's prosperity and what Terrebine had told him of Joy's new ring. Then the thoughts died in Ragan, and he slept.

Two days in Cottonwood and he wondered if he had made a mistake in coming back. He had spent a day renewing acquaintances about town; Andy Julian had been in from Wing J, also Dana Walgamott. They all welcomed him. But nobody needed a rider or knew of a ranch that did. It was all very vague, yet clear to Ragan that he no longer looked like a puncher worth his wages.

What did a cowhand do when that time came to him, usually from advancing age? He cooked for some outfit, or wrangled or swamped for a saloon or got a job carrying mail. Or turned outlaw. Anger grew bright in Ragan, a resentment that once he would have considered unjustified. Only he, himself, knew of the driving will in him that would not admit defeat nor handicap nor demotion. The John Day had simply accepted what he could not—or would not until he died.

There was a dance in the lodge hall Saturday night. Although it meant a chance to see the few men he had missed, Ragan stayed away. It wasn't all because he couldn't face the men who had seen and heard him and, one way or another, turned him down. Joy would be at the dance and so, probably, would Nancy Hanna and other ranch girls he had known. He kept out of the saloons as well, instead taking a bottle of whiskey to his hotel room.

He sat beside a flickering lamp, drinking and smoking until the bottle was half empty. It didn't make him drunk. His mind stayed cold, his spirits unlifted, and he was a tunnel through which ran endless, brooding thoughts. He was face to face with a fact, a painful truth, one a man would keep buried if he could.

The life in a country was fluid. Let a man be out of it a while, and his place was filled, and it became as if he had never occupied that place at all. He could return, but not to his old place. That was gone—in the region and the minds of its people and the hearts of its women. Unless he came back impressively, triumphantly. That Chance Ragan had not been able to do.

Because somebody had shot his horse to murder him, killing not the body but the life, the spirit. That was worse than murder, and the one who did it could not die hard enough.

This thinking stopped abruptly when somebody's knuckles hit Ragan's door. He called a curt command and watched the door swing open.

Angel Younts stood framed there, paused, with a hand on the knob. His hat was set precisely on his hairless head and it stayed there. Younts grinned then, and came on in, closing the door.

"Howdy, Chance," he said. "How come you ain't at the shindig?"

"Why aren't you?"

"The same reason you ain't. Who'd dance with me? I never did have any he-beauty, and you sure got yours knocked off."

Ragan put down his glass very slowly. He nearly rose from his chair but settled back. Younts came on across the room and dropped his weight onto the edge of the bed. He was big without actual height, a blocky man who somehow managed to move with the lightness of a cat. He wore a gun, which few men did in Cottonwood.

He had a ranch in the high breaks of the middle river fork, where the wild horses ran and, with the broncos, the human wild-lings. Younts was suspected of many crimes, but a free man because he had more cunning than those who would have brought him to time.

"We're two of a kind now," Younts was saying. "Cut-backs. Culls."

"Why—God damn you."

"Take it easy," Younts said, with a wave of the hand. "You ain't found a job, have you? Mebbe you guessed what they're saying, Ragan. You look like hell, and you're turning boozer. A man can see it's gone outta you. All the spit and vinegar that used to make Chance Ragan quite a hombre hereabouts."

"Why'd you come here?" Ragan demanded. "To pick a fight with me? Somebody figure a better job could be done of killing me, now?"

"You're already killed. Ain't you?" Younts laughed.

"Who sent you—Terrebine?"

"It happens he did. He's got a job for you. He figures he owes you something."

"Doing what?"

"A job with my trail crew. Buying again, the way you used to, and driving to the mining camps. It'd be your old work, with one difference. Me—I'm the boss in the buying and delivering department. Not you, no more."

25

Ragan came to a rocking stand. For a moment he watched Younts in a sickening humiliation. He couldn't throw the man out, the way he had started to do. He couldn't even knock the hat off Yount's head. Younts knew that. Laughter, cold as winter light, still brightened his pale eyes.

The man pulled out tobacco, selected a paper and applied himself to roll a cigarette. He let the temper spew in Ragan and run out. He knew men. He could jab them painfully or tickle them pleasantly and, if they were tractable, use them freely.

"Terrebine got me out of the cattle company," Ragan said raggedly. "Why should he take me back?"

Younts made wrinkles where his eyebrows should have been "He ain't offering to take you back into the company. What give you that notion? He's only offered a cowhand's job. You want it?"

"Ah," Ragan breathed. "Joy tried to get Judd to offer a job to me. But Arch can't be as independent with her as Judd can. Younts, tell the man where he can put his job. And you and the Terrebine Cattle Company with it."

"And Joy Kildane?" Younts asked softly.

"Get outta here, Younts!" Ragan roared.

Angel Younts only laughed. Then he dropped his cigarette on the carpet and walked out. He left a man half-berserk behind him.

Ragan finished the whiskey. When the bottle was empty he could scarcely walk but still was not drunk the way a man wanted to get when he drank. He could hear the music from the dance. His mind pictured the swinging couples, and he remembered Younts' calling him a cut-back, a cull. The man had wanted to needle and hurt. But there had been a basis for what he said. Hadn't that been proved by Joy, herself?

He still had a few dollars in his pocket. He stayed on in Cottonwood until room-rent and whiskey had used it up. He hated the inertia that had come down upon him. But something had let go in his brain during Younts' visit. Something that had shaped and made him a man. He didn't know what it was. But the thing was torn in two, and he couldn't mend it, and each day he cared less that he could not.

He wasn't concerned the morning he found himself dead broke, save that he retained the pride to move out of the hotel while he could still square up. He slept in the town corral, that night, cursing the hostler who tried to run him off. He awakened with sun in his eyes, not hungry but clawed with thirst.

There wasn't money now for whiskey, and his mind went oddly to the moonshiners who made blue ruin back in the hills. Four-bit liquor. Rot-gut. The kind of booze a tramp had to drink if he was too proud to mooch in the bars. Ragan thought of Poker Annie then, and his resolve never to be like her, and he laughed.

He climbed to his feet, a tall, gaunt figure with straw and chaff on his clothes. His eyes were red-streaked and truculent, while his cheeks were stiff with black beard. He knew how he looked, and felt worse.

The hostler came out of the feed barn and said, "If you'll spend it on breakfast instead of tanglefoot, I'll give you a chance to earn a dollar." Tobacco juice had made a stain down one side of the man's sharp chin. He gummed the chew while he waited to be answered.

"How?" Ragan asked, when he got on top his fighting temper.

The man pointed to a pitchfork. Ragan nodded and went to work, cleaning the corral. He did it thoroughly, although his splitting head was unbearable. The hostler didn't bother to stop him until he had more than earned the money. Then he tossed Ragan a dollar with a look of skepticism. He squirted a post with brown juice and walked back into the stable.

Ragan went down to the creek with the money in his pocket and for the moment forgotten. The look on the man's face hurt in him like a ruptured organ. It was the kind of look he might have given Poker Annie, but he hadn't. He'd touched his hat to her, called her "ma'am." He'd had a drink with her, cheered her up a little. He hadn't known it, then, but must have sensed how close he was to being beaten by life.

They tried to cut my leg off and I still got it, he reflected. Now they're trying to cut my pride out, and I won't stand for that, either. In that moment anger seared the defeat out of him.

He filled his belly with the creek's cold water, but it only cramped him. Afterward he stretched out under a cottonwood and tried to rest again. Sleep came only when he stilled his mind wilfully and kept it from stirring up its black thoughts.

He awakened with the realization that somebody had touched and now was shaking his shoulder. He lay face down,

27

his head on his arms. He breathed a curse and refused to look up. Then a voice spoke, a girl's.

"Chance—wake up."

If it had been the voice of Joy, Ragan wouldn't have sat up so quickly.

"Nancy," he said, and his mouth stayed open.

"Hello, Chance," Nancy Hanna answered.

She had dropped to her knees and remained there, regarding him intently. Her hair was yellow, her cheeks tanned, and her eyes the deepest brown in the country. Her shoulders were straight, her waist trim, and the plainness of her green blouse showed him a woman's roundness.

"The man at the corral said you'd come down here," she resumed. "Either to fish or feed the fishes. The things I've been hearing about you."

"Where's Pace?" Suddenly Ragan wanted to see that friendly man again. In spite of his disgraceful condition, he was glad to see Nancy.

"Dad's home," she said. "I came to town alone. To get you, Chance. We heard you've been on a tear. Now, let down your hackles. That's your business. Dad wants to see you but couldn't come himself. So he sent me to bring you to Ladder."

"To feed me?"

"Cut that out," she snapped. "I brought you a horse. Say the word, and I'll lead it back to Wildcat Creek with its saddle empty."

Even if she had tried, she couldn't have said a better thing to him.

He climbed to his feet, and she came up lightly. She wasn't small, but he made her seem so with his stringy height. Her eyes, regarding him somberly, again were casual, friendly.

She had seen men at their worst and hadn't let it blind her to their best. A man's whiskers, his sweat, his passions and weaknesses held no offense for Nancy. She was an honest woman, a sincere one, and a realist. Pace had known what Chance Ragan needed.

She turned and started walking, and Ragan tramped along beside her. He felt his pride coming back to him. He felt a lot better.

4

NANCY HAD left her horse in front of the Roundup. It was a sleek, smallish black. A heavier roan stood beside it, carrying Hanna's Ladder brand on its shoulder.

She looked up at Ragan. "You want to bring your war bag?"

He bristled. "Now, look here—"

"All right—all right. But it will be a long ride back to get it, if you take the job Dad and Kitch Dunsan have in mind for you."

"Kitch Dunsan? What's that fuzz-cheeked kid got to do with it?"

Nancy flushed. "Kitch is twenty-two. And running Spade. I wrote you his father died last winter. Kitch and us are making our roundup now. The only ones in the country who are. Where's your stuff?"

"At the corral."

"We'll stop for it." He said nothing at the way she had decided the question for him.

Within minutes they were riding south from Cottonwood, moving at a fast trot along the meanders of the Wildcat, its benches banked high above them. Nancy had made no purchases in town, obviously had come only to fetch him home with her. That interested him, yet it made him wary. Pace couldn't afford hired help, even if he had need of it. The need was doubtful, for Nancy was as good as a man in the saddle, even as she was better than most women in a kitchen. Yet she seemed very young to him, somewhere around the age of Kitch Dunsan.

But Spade was another matter. In the old days Frank Dunsan had kept a couple of hands besides his redheaded son who now seemed to be running the outfit. Ragan hadn't yet seen anybody from Spade, and they were holding roundup. Hope rose in him.

Where the creek bent north, the trail climbed out of the gorge. They came at once into rugged country and were dwarfed by the mountains. To the left ran the high breaks of the middle John Day, crowding the sky. They were staggered rises, climbing in stepbacks for as high as three thousand feet. The flaming rock of their lava construction was a striking red in the sunshine. On all the slopes and headlands grew the yellow pine of the Blue Mountains.

Ragan sat loose in the saddle, beginning to throw off his headache. With it he got rid of the feeling of filth from his long drunk and lack of grooming. Nancy was quiet for her, and he watched her often and thought of her steadily.

He didn't think she had launched herself on any mission of salvation. She had been sent to bring him, and he remembered her flush when he spoke of the callowness of Kitch Dunsan. The two buttons had grown up on neighboring ranches, had always run together. But now there probably was a much more mature feeling between them. Kitch was blind if he didn't have his loop on her already. From her blush he had an idea Nancy was willing.

The trail began to twist and ask more of the horses. They crossed the divide and started to descend into the country she called home. Presently they were crossing the interlocked flats of wild meadow that made the hill country good cattle range. Two hours later they rode down on Ladder's headquarters.

The ranch buildings lay at the foot of a spur of the Blues. The house was small, a starter log cabin to which additions had been made of milled lumber. It stood on the edge of a brawling creek, and out from the site ran a big feeding flat. Ragan had come here many times in the old days, and it was here that Hanna had brought the half-dead man he found in the snowdrift.

The larger Spade outfit stretched south of Ladder, and beyond Spade sprawled the yet greater holdings of Judd Kildane. The three outfits held most of the foothill range, while westward lay the other spreads of the upper middle fork.

If Pace had been too busy with roundup to come for Ragan, he gave no sign of it. He was seated on the front porch of the house, obviously waiting for the newcomers. He got up and hitched his pants as he came down the steps, walking in a cowman's twisting, wide-legged stride.

"You look like hell," he said in greeting.

Ragan gave him a long study and said, "You sent good bait for me, Pace. So feed me good, now that I'm here."

"We'll eat," Pace agreed. "Then go over to see Kitch."

"He got a real job or are you two making it?"

"Both. Light down and rest your saddle. I'll put up the hammerheads."

Ragan stepped out of leather, tireder than he wanted the Hannas to notice. Nancy swung down lightly, smiled an invitation and led him toward the house. He turned around when halfway to the porch, aware of something he was going to do before he entered their home.

His old range clothes were in his roll, together with a razor and what else he needed. He called, "Be back," after Nancy and strode off. He got his kit, left Hanna to finish with the horses, and struck out for the creek in the brush-screened distance.

There he stripped and bathed, afterward standing naked in the bright sunshine and feeling its heat while he shaved. He dressed, combed his hair, and sat for a moment smoking a cigarette. Later he wrinkled his nose at his filthy, discarded clothing. Scooping a hole in the sand bar, he buried the garments.

At that moment he heard Pace bawl, "Come and get it!" and went back to the house.

He ate with a relish that surprised him, the first time he had enjoyed food in months. It was the exercise, the mountain air and more than that, here was one place on the John Day where nothing had changed. Much better than that, it was a place where he was not considered to be much changed himself.

Pace and Ragan saddled fresh horses after the meal, and made the ride to Spade. The ranch was situated the same as Ladder except that it had a bunkhouse for its riders. As Pace had done, Kitch Dunsan also expected Ragan. A redhead, he was heavily freckled, and he had a quick grin. He looked more mature than Ragan remembered. The responsibility he had inherited with the ranch had done that to him, apparently.

"You couldn't have picked a better time to show up, Chance," he said, shaking hands. "You and Pace come into the office. I got a bottle. We both got a proposition to put to you."

"You don't need a rider?" Ragan asked suspiciously.

"Not on Spade. This is special."

"Look—" Ragan began, pulling himself taller.

Kitch grinned at him. "Just one big sore thumb, ain't you? Keep a dally on that temper, and I'll tell you about the thing. If you take the job, you won't ever have tackled anything

31

tougher. It would help us, and mebbe the whole country, like nothing I can think of. But let's set and drink while we talk it over."

They were presently seated in battered chairs in what Ragan remembered as Frank Dunsan's office, off the main room of the house. It was a small, plain place, its walls of uncovered boards long since turned brown by time. There was a desk and safe, and an out-of-date calendar furnished sometime in the remote past by a Dalles City merchant. There was a dirty, blindless window whose panes were nearly impervious to light.

"You know our Squabble Creek line camp, Chance," Kitch said as he poured whiskey. "How'd you like to squat on it through this coming winter?"

"Me?" said Ragan.

"You and a few steers," Kitch said. "Pace and Dad cooked the scheme up, without trying to make a job for anybody. They meant to put me out there, at first. Now Dad's gone, and I can't do it. So when Pace told me you were headed home, we knew we had the man we need."

"Then you're kind of freaks in this country."

"Who'd be a better man," Pace said softly, "to tie into the Terrebine Cattle Company?"

That made Ragan sit up straight in his chair, his eyes going bright and narrow.

"Come again," he retorted.

Pace grinned. "You heard me right. Terrebine and Younts are pulling the juiciest rustling job a man ever heard of. We aim to nail 'em for it."

"Rustling?" Ragan gasped.

"That's what you call stealing cattle, ain't it?" Pace enjoyed the shock he had given Ragan. He made himself a cigarette, licked the paper and sealed it. Then he looked at Ragan through squinted eyes. "See why you got horned out of the company?"

"No," said Ragan.

"Could Terrebine have gone in for rustling with you his pardner?"

"Not by a damsite."

"This is plenty big," Pace elaborated. "Me and Kitch's dad got suspicious last spring. Younts and his riders were burning too much moonlight to look natural. We figured part of it out then. But the hell of it is, their scheme's blamed near catchproof. We can't do a thing about it at present."

32

"Well, I'm no range detective," Ragan said.

"The rustling makes it a cinch, you jughead," Pace retorted, "that Terrebine was behind you getting bushwhacked. Don't that give you a stake in the thing? On top of that, it would help me and Kitch if we could run stuff on Squabble Creek next winter. If you're on, we can make up the cut while we're holding roundup."

"If it's got anything to do with that bushwhacking, I'm on," Ragan said. "Ain't Arch buying any cattle now?"

"Oh, the usual quantity. But if his butcher shops kept books, they'd show a turnover twice as big. Chance, we've seen plenty of sign. We know damned well the new company's crooked as a rail fence."

"Angel Younts offered me a job," Ragan said. "If they dealt me out so they could turn crooked, why'd they take me in again?"

"Angel did that?" Pace asked, surprised. The shadowy light made the grey of his temples seem more vivid.

Ragan nodded. "Still," he mused, "he went out of his way to get under my skin with digs about my condition. I had a feeling somebody'd pressured Arch into making some kind of offer. Maybe Younts just saw to it that I turned it down. What have you seen?"

"Evidence that he drifted cattle across the Squabble Creek flat all through the winter, after Spade had pulled out its line rider. When sign showed up, we laid for them and seen the moving cattle."

"Why didn't you latch onto the sons, then and there?"

"They're too slick to go off half-cocked with. You know how a legitimate meat business runs. Most ranchers like the kind of market the mines make. I did myself, back in your time. Man don't need to hold anything but a calf roundup. There's just one chance a year for him to tally his herd.

"And Terrebine's taking advantage of it. He gets a bill of sale for the cattle Younts picks up and pays for. But the steers never get bunched up much, just go off to some mining camp in dabs. It would take a wizard to prove that Younts and his riders have rustled on the same brand. Any cut you might ask an accounting for, they'd have a bill of sale to show. Sounds more complicated than it is, and that's what's stumped me and Kitch."

"And you figure I'm your wizard?"

"I'm telling you why we didn't call in the law and put a stop to it. We've got to catch 'em redhanded, and we think

33

Squabble Creek's the place to do it. Someplace they're bound to have a weakness. We've got to find and use it."

Ragan was convinced that the two cowmen were riding the right trail. Their suspicions were only that, but they put sense into what had happened to himself the previous winter. If it could be proved, it would make certain what he now could only guess, that Terrebine had been behind that bushwhacking.

Ragan wanted to prove the theory; he was going to do it. The decision came with its old snapping swiftness. He was getting his teeth in things again.

He said, "What do I live on all winter? Your beef?"

"The camp's stocked," Kitch said. "Meant to put one of my boys out there, anyhow. I'll be glad not to have to spare him. There'll be regular riding pay for you, Chance, if you'll also look after the stuff me and Pace want to winter there. And you can fix the place up. Lots of work needed. Me and Pace'll split the bill."

Ragan searched the young rancher's face, moved by his fear of being helped out of pity. He saw nothing to disturb him in Kitch's open countenance. Pace Hanna also looked guileless. They were practical, neighborly men, only helping him and each other.

Ragan's grin came again. "Then it's a deal. When do I start to work?"

"You can move up there today," Kitch said. Pace shoved back his hat and smiled. Youth and freckles, and gray temples, and a grim and stringy man. Something flowed between them that was clean and good, stubborn and honest, clear-eyed and unafraid.

But Ragan was not yet ready to tie himself down on Squabble Creek, not when he had this new insight into the activities of Terrebine and Younts.

He said, "Terrebine made me that offer, through Angel, of a job riding for the company. What if I went over to Younts' place and told him I'll take it? If he crawfished, we'd have another sign you've got it figured right. If he decided he had to make good the bluff, that might lead to something useful, too. There's no rush about getting somebody on Squabble Creek, is there?"

"Not for two-three weeks, anyhow," Kitch admitted. "But it would spoil the caper to let 'em know we suspect something. It might gravel your pride, Chance, but the stunt would work better if they thought we'd only made you a winter job. That's what it would look like. We ain't wintered cattle up there for a long while."

"I know that," Ragan said, "and I won't spoil it. You let me take my own look at things, that's all."

"All right," Pace said. "But you stay at Ladder tonight. Nancy expects you to."

Kitch said, "Any prospect of me getting invited to supper, Pace? I ain't tried Nancy's cooking for several days."

"Come on," Pace said heartily. "The more the merrier."

Ragan spent a rare pleasant evening, that night at Ladder. He remembered Pace's wife and her last illness. Overnight, her death had made Nancy change from a teen-aged girl to a ranch woman, with not only a house to run but a range job to fill between times. Yet he failed to see where the responsibility had taken anything out of her. She looked as fresh and pretty as she had when he first knew her as a girl with yellow pigtails and an abundance of vitality and spirit.

During that evening, he discerned the deep bond between her and Kitch Dunsan that he had suspected. They seemed to think alike, to talk alike. They were always referring matters to each other as they chatted, mutually dependent in their thinking.

"Remember, Kitch?" she would ask.

"Ain't that so, Nancy?" he would inquire.

Sometimes they had only to look at one another and nod to underscore a full, tacit understanding. It was a nice relationship, Ragan thought, the outgrowth of a childhood spent together, active, aggressive and clean. It was a point in his own favor that they cared to count him a friend.

Kitch left after supper, when the talk at the table broke up. Nancy went into the kitchen to wash the dishes. Ragan took a seat in the sitting room, drawing out tobacco and offering an opinion.

"One of these times, Pace, you're going to lose a fine cook."

Pace gave him a close glance. "To Kitch? Not them two. They've knowed each other too long and too well."

"What's wrong with that?"

Pace grinned. "Well, it's a situation where the marriage bug has a hard time getting a foothold."

5

AFTER AN early breakfast Ragan asked Pace for the loan of the horse he had ridden out from Cottonwood. He got out his shell belt and Colt .45 and strapped them on. He slung his roll across the cantle and tied it down. He promised Pace that, whatever happened, he would be back within the two weeks. Then he rode out alone.

He knew the country as well as any man did. Back in the days of Terrebine and Ragan, his work had taken him to all the ranches in the valley. He had learned every foot of the main trails as well as the shortcuts. He headed for the backland ranch of Angel Younts, riding cross-country.

At the end of two hours' traveling he drew in sight of Younts' Fork. Riding down to headquarters, he saw that many alterations had been made to fit the ranch into Terrebine's new handling system. The feeding flat had been cut into several pastures. He knew that the steers bought in the valley were brought here to be sorted and held, as necessary, before going on to the scattered slaughterhouses and retail outlets.

The buildings of the place were as ramshackle as in the old days. Ragan saw that he had been lucky. He observed men moving about headquarters—he had been afraid that he would not find Younts home.

The man was with a group at the horse corral when Ragan rode up. They all watched in surprise, silent and surly. He tipped a casual nod, his eyes on Younts.

"Howdy, Angel," he said. "You still got that job for me?"

He couldn't have drawn a more pronounced reaction from the bunch if he'd offered to lick their boots. Younts' mouth dropped open. He lifted the flat of his hand and dragged it along the line of his jaw. Ragan didn't know why. There were no whiskers.

"You turned it down," he grunted.

Ragan grinned. "A man can change his mind quick, sometimes. I'm busted. I got to have a job, and nobody else has

36

made an offer. It looks like you called the tune, the other night. I'm in with the culls and cut-backs."

"Meanin' us?"

"That's what you called us both, Angel. How about it? You got a job for me, or were you only talking through your hat?"

"Well, I'll be damned," Younts said. He was lost in secret thinking for an instant, then he reached a decision that was reflected in his lashless eyes. "Well, the job's still yours if you want it. Ready to go to work?"

"When you say the word."

"Then throw your stuff in the bunkhouse. Right off, you can take a cut of beef over to Dixie for me."

"Today?"

"Soon as we get it made up. We were starting to cut it out when you hit here."

There were cattle in the corrals. They were shorthorns, the stocky beef breed being established on the Oregon desert. Younts said that his boys would do the cutting while Ragan got together a pack outfit. The round trip would keep him trailing about three days.

Younts stayed with Ragan while he made up the pack and, afterward, snaked a pony out of the horse corral. Fork used a lot of mustangs, for the runs of the wild bunch were nearby. The pack horse Younts pointed out for Ragan to rope was of that breed.

Finally Younts said, "Got any ideas about that bushwhack last winter?"

The question was as startling to Ragan as his own request for a job must have been to Younts. He flung the man a quick, close stare.

Bluntly he said, "It could have been you, wanting to get into the company and knowing I wouldn't stand for it as long as I was a pardner. It could have been Terrebine wanting things all in his own hands. Or it could have been a moonshiner taking me for a lawman. Those are the possibilities. What do you think, Angel?"

"I always figured it was moonshiners," Younts said easily. "They're thicker'n fleas on a dog's back around here. I got a hunch some of them are starting sidelines. There's been rustling sign lately."

"That a fact?" Again Ragan had trouble hiding his surprise at the man's bluntness.

"Thought I'd better tell you," Younts said. "You're going over the Dixie Creek pass. That's the kind of wild country where a man could lose his steers. Don't get caught napping."

"Not the second time," Ragan said, and meant it heartily.

He was puzzled as to why Younts had wanted to leave that thought with him. He remembered the deep contemplation that had gone on in the man before he decided to make good on his offer of a job. Ragan thought he knew already why he was being sent off to Dixie the first thing. That would give Younts time to get in touch with Terrebine and find out how to handle this unexpected development.

You're damned right I'll stay awake, Ragan told himself.

He trailed in midmorning with a beef cut of fifty head. The steers would give him little trouble, and it was mainly a matter of escorting them to the holding pen of the Dixie butcher. But the trek meant crossing primitive country that shoved high against the sky. It meant days in which he was not apt to encounter anybody at all. That angle could give him plenty of trouble, and he knew it well.

Settled on the trail, he began to relax except for his steady alertness against some unexpected development. Riding did not tire him now as much as it had at first. Working cattle was so ingrained in him it was second nature. The wild country was invigorating and seemed to strengthen him.

The route took him through a system of joined mountain flats that rose higher and higher toward the ridgeline of the main Blues. In view of his late start from Fork, he pressed on through midday, intending to keep going until he found a good place to camp for the night.

As he rose higher, the yellow pine of the mountains crowded close. Some of the canyons he had to follow were plenty rough. But he was used to such going and had no trouble handling the cattle. The ease with which he did it was gratifying.

Since he had never traveled this way directly from Younts' Fork, there were times when he was puzzled as to his bearings. But the position of the sun and the length of its shadows told him what he needed to know. When the shade began to stretch notably, he came to a creek with a long, flat meadow. He let the steers drink and scatter to graze. Then he set up a simple camp.

Supper was plain, of coffee, bacon and cold biscuits brought from Fork. Afterward he rode a circle about the little mountain meadow. When he found nothing to disturb him, he returned to camp, unsaddled and picketed his horse. Mountain coolness

38

had begun to flow in with the weakening light. Darkness came on full and sudden.

Ragan freshened the fire and sat by it, smoking and drinking the last of the coffee. The warning sense he had felt at Fork began to nag at him again. He would reach Dixie tomorrow and get back to Fork the following day, making this his only trail camp. If trouble came, the most likely time would be tonight.

His interest was not solely in the matter of meeting and surviving it. If it came, he wanted to know who had brought it. That had been his whole purpose in making the bold move of hiring out to Younts in spite of the man's taunting insult.

He let the fire die, finally, then scattered the last of the coals. Where his riding and pack saddles lay, he spread out his blankets. Then he brought rocks from the creek and placed them between the blankets. When he was done arranging them, they gave from the distance the impression of a man's body in the bed. Afterward he moved out through the cottonwood of the creek and found a seat where he could watch the whole of the little meadow.

The stars emerged, a blaze of brightness across the depthless black. With them the night air grew colder. Yet Ragan felt that he could afford the sacrifice of his blankets and of sleep. He remained warily expectant although the hours wore on with nothing disturbing the quietness of the mountain flat. He began to wonder if he had figured the whole thing wrong—then it came, sudden and with full impact.

The warning was in the earth, itself, the beat of horses' hoofs slowly but unmistakably drumming up. His lips pulled back from his teeth as he got to his feet. He moved over a little, taking station with his back to the trunk of a cottonwood. He still could see the flat in its entirety. His gun was in his grip, but he did not mean to use it unless cornered and forced to do so.

Presently he saw two moving dots in the distant starshine. They were horses coming in along the trail he had himself established. They came at a trot, and Ragan could tell when the riders detected the bedded steers, for the horses slowed abruptly. The oncomers would know where to find his camp, for it would be somewhere on the creek and probably under the trees.

Ragan watched them cut over to the stream at a point somewhat down from him. He threw a checking glance at his camp. The picketed horse marked its location plainly.

He waited for them to take the bait he had set out so carefully in that rock-filled bed.

The horsemen dismounted at a point still downstream from him. He watched that movement with a bated breath. Soon he could neither see nor hear them, for they were extremely cautious. He lost all track of them until, suddenly, the crack of a pistol rent the silence. The nightriders emptied their guns into the camp. They shot at what they thought to be a sleeping Ragan.

His first instinct was to jump them, then and there, before they had reloaded their weapons. But he discarded that. It was more important to discover where they would take the steers in the guise of the rustling moonshiners Angel Younts had so carefully mentioned.

Ragan feared that the would-be killers would move in on the camp to check the results of their shooting. But they did not do it. They seemed to be in a rush, for they cut their mounts boldly onto the flat, driving across it. When he considered it safe, he moved back to his own horse, saddled it hastily and rose up to leather. He turned along the creek, still keeping to the brush and watching what took place in the open.

He saw that they were getting around behind the cut of cattle. They meant to move it back along the trail it had covered that same day. Going home to Fork, probably, and that was a question Ragan wanted to answer beyond doubt. If that was what happened, he would have proof of everything he had come to suspect with Pace and Kitch. But, like them, he would keep his suspicions quiet until they were in a position to expose the whole rotten thing.

The two gunmen had no trouble getting the steers on their way. Ragan followed at a cautious distance, so certain as to where they would go that he had only to keep safely out of sight and ride. He was tempted once to try to get ahead and see if he could identify the men, but that looked risky.

At the end of an hour's trailing, he received a surprise. Abruptly the rustlers left the home trail, turning up a little stream that cut across a flat. This puzzled Ragan, and in the night he had lost track of his exact position. They were turning right. He followed doggedly, less certain about it all than he had been.

It seemed to him that he went on for three or four hours more, always careful. Then, with little warning, he found himself on a rimrock that rose for some sixty feet above a mountain coulee larger than any he had seen in that part of the country. Its appearance there had not surprised him so much as the fact that cattle in great numbers grazed in it. He knew that his hunch and ensuing patience had brought him to the main rustlers' hideout.

He was even less desirous now of betraying to the night-riders the fact that they had been followed. He waited quietly where he was, not even daring to smoke. He saw nothing more of the horsemen. Once they had thrown the new steers in here, they seemed really to have headed for home.

That could be Fork or any other shady hangout in this part of the country.

6

WHEN DAYLIGHT came, Ragan got a better look from his viewpoint on the rimrock. He still had not dared to ride down into the open to see what he could learn about the brands on the steers out there. But with good light he could tally the hidden herd, which he estimated at nearly four hundred head. He made out enough brands on the closer cattle to know that they had come from far and wide.

The operation was bigger than had been anticipated by Hanna and Dunsan. The brands showed that the rustlers were working the country as far west as Crooked River, north to the Umatilla and east to the Powder. The thing was so big that it sobered Ragan. The profits would also be big enough to incite murder—past, present and future.

The night riders must have come from Fork.

He took his bearings by day, yet still was not sure as to where he was. So he had to follow his own tracks until he came to the cattle trail he himself had blazed previously. He knew he could get back to this place, then, and he started on for Fork.

It was obvious he had escaped being murdered only by his own foresight. Now he had two problems to consider. His return unhurt would arouse serious suspicions on Fork. Yet if he failed to return, and his body was not found at the mountain camp, suspicion would be even stronger.

41

He decided it would be wise to show himself to some neutral person, between the time of that vicious attack and his return to Younts' ranch. Otherwise there was nothing to keep Younts from making good the effort there, and transporting his body back to the deserted trail camp. It still could be claimed that moonshiners had done the killing and rustling. Therefore, as Ragan came down into the lower country, he cut over toward Susanville.

One of the boom camps built in haste after the placer strike throughout the Blues, Susanville showed femininity only in its name. As rough and ready as the toughest of cowtowns, the place was frequented but rarely by local cowmen. Reaching there in midafternoon, Ragan figured he had only to talk with somebody here, and let that fact be known on Fork, to escape being made the victim of the murder trap even yet.

He still had no money to buy himself a drink or the meal that he wanted badly. But he could ask some questions of a bartender, and there might even be somebody around he had known in the old days. Then, coming onto the dumpy camp street, his problem was solved for him.

He saw Joy Kildane come out of a mercantile with a package on her arm. She saw him in the same moment, and her face lighted up.

She called, "Hello! You're the last person I expected to see here."

"And you," he returned, swinging his horse over to the edge of the walk. "Heading home? If so, we can ride a ways together."

"I am," she said.

Her horse was at the store hitchrack. She stuffed her purchase into a saddle pocket, then rose lightly to the leather.

It was a good break, Ragan reflected as they rode out of camp together. He decided against telling her about his experience in the mountains, which would bring questions he did not want to answer. It was enough that she had seen him here since it happened.

When they entered the sage of the countryside, Joy broke the silence.

"I should have corrected Arch, the other day in Canyon City," she said wistfully, "when he bragged about the ring. It's quite true that he's having one made and talked me into looking at it. But you'll notice that he still hasn't put it on my finger."

"What's holding you back?"

42

"Several things. I'm tired of beating around the bush about it, Chance. Once I thought we were going to mean a lot to each other. I sort of liked the idea. I think you did, too."

"Things have changed."

She turned her head, and her eyes searched him. "I don't see why it's so final. I've been thinking about your bitterness toward Arch. Maybe you're right. You're the one who made the cattle company pay, until he got the monopoly on the mining-camp markets."

And started rustling a good part of the beef he sells in them, Ragan thought bitterly. Aloud, he said, "I reckon that's water under the bridge now, Joy."

"I think you ought to break that monopoly, Chance."

"Me? What with?"

"My help."

He swung in the saddle to stare at her. "Just how?"

"I could loan you the money. And when you've crowded Arch into a corner, I'll help you buy him out."

"You're that done with him?"

"It depends on you, entirely."

"In short, you don't know yet which horse you ought to bet on. Me, if you can be sure I'll win. But you can't be sure, so you're hedging."

"Did I say that?" she cried, and her eyes were suddenly furious.

"All but."

"I was only trying to help you."

"To reach a place where you'd be satisfied to marry me. Thanks, Joy. But I don't want that. And I don't like the idea that you can't let go of either one of us."

"Why must you be so impossible?"

He said nothing at all.

For a moment she stared straight forward. When still he did not speak, she struck her horse a blow with her quirt and was gone, riding ahead of him. He made no attempt to catch up. Yet a sunk feeling was in his middle as he jogged on.

The disaster that had struck him down had changed his feeling for a great many people, in a sense separating the dross from the gold. Once he had wanted her desperately, and he guessed that he still did. The barriers that kept rising between them did not lessen that fundamental, deep-burning desire to have her, to know her delights—they only frus-

43

trated it, so that a torment must fill him always, when he was with her or apart.

It was nearly dark when he rode into Fork. Although he kept his face impassive, there was a cool glint of satisfaction in his eyes. A man came to the bunkhouse door at the sound of his arriving horse to start hard then let out a gasp.

"By God—it's Ragan!"

"Anything wrong with being him?" Ragan inquired.

"But—but you couldn't of got to Dixie and back so soon. What happened?"

"I had a little trouble. Where's Angel?"

Younts had already appeared on the porch of the house. For a moment he only stood there looking across the yard at Ragan. He didn't speak while Ragan rode over and dismounted at the porch steps.

Then Younts said, "Well, what's the story?" His voice was a little tight.

"I lost the steers," Ragan said calmly. "A good thing you warned me, Angel, or I'd have been ventilated in my sleep. Two sons-of-bitches from somewhere shot the hell outta my camp."

"Didn't you put up a fight?" Younts asked.

"Not me. What chance would I stand against two of 'em? I laid low, Angel, and afterward trailed them far enough I can show the sheriff where to look for the steers."

Younts made a betraying start. "The sheriff? You didn't report it, did you?"

"Figured that was your place or Arch's."

Younts could not help showing relief. "Yeah. We'll take care of it. You better get yourself some sleep."

"Meal first. I come home by way of Susanville but lacked the dinero to buy something to eat."

"You were in Susanville?"

"Didn't stop. Run into Joy Kildane, and we rode part way home together."

From the sharp look Younts gave him. Ragan realized that the man's mind had run along the lines anticipated. But Younts knew now that he could make nothing further out of that mountain shooting. He questioned Ragan perfunctorily as to the place and manner of the attack. Yet it was so idle and incurious that Ragan knew the man didn't really need to be told. Younts said he would send a man out to bring back the abandoned packhorse. He committed himself to nothing else.

44

Ragan ate cold food set up for him by a grumpy cook. Afterward he agreed with Younts that he needed sleep. His body ached from fatigue. He went to the bunkhouse and found it to be the kind of boar's nest to be expected on so crumby a spread. There was a bunk that did not seem to be occupied, with blankets folded at its foot. He made up a bed, undressed and turned in with his six-gun under the pillow. His sleep was neither deep nor refreshing. He knew that he had entered a situation of deep jeopardy. These men had proved their desire to get rid of him. That seemed to confirm his belief that what happened last winter had been brought off by the same men. He had hinted to Younts his knowledge of the coulee and its stolen cattle. This kept churning in Ragan, engendering a mixed hatred and apprehension that would not be dissipated until a final decision had come.

He slept through the short remainder of that day, then on through the night, his weakened body trying to regain its energy. That seemed agreeable to Younts, for Ragan was not disturbed. When he aroused at daylight the crew was starting to get up. Younts had four men here. But there would be others working for him.

On hand were two men Ragan had known slightly in the past, Squint Lister and Stub Nelson. Neither was reassuring looking. Ragan washed at the bunkhouse bench with them, then ate his breakfast. He was smoking a cigarette in the yard when Younts came out of the big house, apparently to issue day orders. Yet Ragan straightened, not seeing Younts as much as the man with him.

Arch Terrebine gave him an impersonal glance, but the two walked straight toward Ragan, who realized he faced a crisis. Terrebine nodded coolly as they came up. On the mouth of Younts was the hint of a smile. The others, curious, formed about.

"Well, Ragan," said Younts, "Arch don't think we need to call the law in on that rustling. It was moonshiners, sure as hell. I'm sending the boys along the sign to run 'em down."

"Don't you want me along?" Ragan asked.

Younts shook his hairless head. "Got a better job for you. One you used to be good at. Squint, you take the boys and ride the sign Ragan made. Just find out where them steers went, then report back, and we'll figure out our next move."

Lister motioned to the other riders, and they all walked off toward the horse corral. Ragan waited, a dryness in his mouth, not liking the look in Terrebine's slate eyes. But Younts, as if in afterthought, followed his men to the corral. Then Ragan realized that this was to give Terrebine a chance for a private word.

The man cleared his throat and looked at Ragan. It was the first time they had been alone together since before the trouble.

He said, "I guess you're sore at me for a couple of reasons, Chance. We might as well square up to it. The cattle idea was mine in the first place, remember. It was me got it going. And I didn't have any money to loan when you were in the hospital. I tried to borrow it for you and couldn't. There just wasn't enough security. The only way I could get money to help you was to take in a new pardner and buy you out."

"It wasn't Younts," Ragan said. "He never had the money to do all you've done since."

"Not Younts," Terrebine agreed. "But an old friend of mine from down in my old home country. That don't matter now. He's a silent pardner and wants it kept that way. I could have explained it better at the time I took up your offer to sell. But I didn't want you to know I was in such a corner."

"That don't even sound good, Arch. It's too damned phony."

The slate eyes were streaked suddenly. The handsome mouth ruled straighter. "Maybe me and Joy help you feel that way. When it comes to a woman, I figure it's every man for himself. You got no reason to resent me wanting her. What man wouldn't? And I've got as much reason to be sore as you have. She's a hard one to dab a loop on, and your coming back's upset things for me plenty."

"Fine," said Ragan. "That's to the credit side of the ledger."

"Anyhow, we understand each other."

"Not that you puzzled me much, Arch," Ragan retorted. "Not ever."

Terrebine's eyes probed deeper, then he shrugged and walked off.

Squint Lister rode out, leading the other three riders on a mission as false as Terrebine's effort to account for his actions. They all knew they hadn't fooled him. They were only trying to keep him as uncertain and off-balance as possible.

When Younts came back he was genial. "If you're caught up on your rest, Ragan," he said, "I got a cut of mustangs in a corral up in the hills. Mean to bust 'em down for our own use here. I'll go with you, and we'll fetch one in."

"Okay," Ragan said, curious as to what-all Younts had in mind.

They roped horses, saddled them and headed out. At the edge of the headquarters flat, they struck into a canyon. They pressed on until they came to a pole corral far in the foothills. It held half a dozen restless wild horses. They were the wiry, shaggy broomtails of the John Day breaks. Ragan saw that Younts' riders had captured a stallion, a beautiful, wicked looking white with its harem.

"We going to try to run them thunderbolts down to headquarters?" Ragan asked.

"Only the stud, and we'll take him down on ropes. I want that white boy for myself, and I want him broke right."

A slow awareness dawned on Ragan. It sharpened quickly into concern.

"Could it be you intend for me to stomp him, Angel?"

"Asked for a job, didn't you? And you used to be one of the best twisters in these parts." Younts underscored the pastness of that qualification and did it with the ghost of a grin.

"But not now?" Ragan said softly.

"We'll see when you climb aboard."

The slurring edge to the man's voice hardened the determination in Ragan. He only shrugged. He'd ride the damned stud horse or die.

They got two catch ropes on the stallion, then half led and half dragged it out of the corral. There it spent five minutes trying to untangle itself. When the effort failed, it wanted to run. The riders let it travel, guiding it along the trail back down to Fork headquarters. In less than an hour they had the mustang in the breaking trap.

It was noon by then. A broken-down old cowhand called Frank did the cooking in a combined cooking and eating space tacked onto the bunkhouse.

Younts said, "Well, Ragan, you better chuck up before you give the devil a little whirl." Again the man let a taunt show in his eyes. He expected Ragan to object to the assignment, for it would take a man in top condition to stay

47

aboard that horse. "The boys have worked with him a little, already. He's ready to fork."

"If I'm going to do it, it'll be on an empty belly," Ragan retorted. "I don't hanker for a ruptured gut."

"Then we'll throw on a saddle," said Younts. "I'll get Frank and Arch to help."

It was hard for Ragan to withhold his objections. But he let Younts walk off and return with Terrebine and the old cook. Younts entered the corral with a catch-rope, forefooted the stallion and brought it down. Frank slipped a blindfold over its eyes, and looked as excited as the other two men. As the horse struggled up it was drawn tight to the snubbing post.

Ragan's jaw muscles bulged but he said nothing as he moved in. He approached the bronco quietly and began to rub its head, neck and back, to help quiet it down. Then he began to use the saddle blanket, getting the animal accustomed to its feel. Finally he began to ease the saddle onto the stallion's back. Then he started to put on the saddle, slowly and with great care. He pulled off the blindfold, loosened the rope and let the *oreana* try to pitch off the empty leather.

There was a grassy lump in his stomach as he watched the effort. The wild stud knew every trick in the book and used it trying to dislodge that empty kak. Each twisting, pitching attempt seemed to give pleasure to the other watchers.

Mebbe they got them a new murder trap, Ragan thought grimly.

He could not bring himself to protest when Younts snubbed the horse in again before it had worked off its devilish energy. The *oreana* made a whistling snort and struck out with bared teeth at Younts. Its pink eyes were wild with fury.

Terrebine said, "Angel, I've got my doubts about this. Maybe Chance was a bronc-twister once. But he's sure not in shape for that fellow now. You better have Stub work him over." The man was not interceding for Ragan. His words were stinging goads.

Younts grinned and looked at Ragan. "It's your say. If you ain't up to it, all right."

"Why goddam' you," Ragan said. He put his foot in the stirrup and went up.

Strangely, the stallion stood motionless for seconds after it had been turned loose. Then it made a series of crow-hopping steps, each one jarring the length of Ragan's sensitive spine. Immediately after that it threw itself into a bucking circle, clear around the big trap.

Dust boiled up to smother Ragan. The beat of hoofs was a lethal drumming in his ears. He used his hat and yelled his challenge and stayed in the saddle. Abruptly the stallion swapped ends, reared and tried to throw itself into a back-fall. Ragan beat down its head with a fist. Again the horse bucked a full circle around the corral.

Ragan knew his weakened leg wouldn't hold him in the saddle very long, even if he could stand the pain of it.

He could have yelled at the men to rope the horse again, he could have hollered 'uncle' and saved himself. He didn't do it. The wily mustang had discovered the surest way to beat the enemy on its back. It crow-hopped, then threw itself up in a cat-back and came down stiff-legged. Each time Ragan felt the blood swell in his nose and ears. His insides seemed to tear loose from their moorings.

The dust was so thick he could no longer see the men who had crowded him into this. Yet from somewhere he mustered the will to stay in the saddle, beating his bad leg and the worst the stallion could do. Experience helped him; he had instinctive timing and balance.

There was a short while in which the stallion seemed to be tiring, in which Ragan dared to hope that he was going to ride it down. But that was swept away in a burst of re-newed and raging effort. Ragan had to grab leather. He was gagging for breath in the dust-fouled air.

Then it happened. He needed the bad leg, and the leg just wasn't there at all. He felt himself coming loose, then being hurled upward, thinking, They'll let the wild devil kill me . . . an accident . . . a beautiful accident at just the right time . . .

Something walloped him, and that was followed by a deep and swirling blackness. Then he knew no more.

7

HE HAD been so certain he was being murdered that he was surprised when he opened his eyes. They had kept the killer horse off him and carried him into the bunkhouse, where he was now stretched out in racking pain. He groaned and, as his vision cleared, looked about.

Younts stood over him, watching down, his hairless head an odd, foreshortened shape. He said, "Well, Ragan, it's too bad. But the only job I got open is bronc stomping. You just ain't the man for it. Not any more."

Ragan was too weak to curse him. He sat up, dizziness assaulting him, a wave of blackness rolling before his eyes. He shook his head, trying to clear his vision. Somehow he got off the bunk and onto his feet.

He stood swaying, having to hold himself upright by a post of the bunk, he stared at Arch Terrebine. The man was seated on a bunkhouse chair, watching with clinical interest, amused. He must have been deeply gratified by what he had seen happen in the trap.

"You're a clever bunch of coyotes!" Ragan panted. He felt like a skeleton of bare, aching bones as he stood there.

He knew they had tried to do more than kill him. They had attacked his very spirit again and hoped to watch it die. That realization was a jet of acid into Ragan's blood, destroying the numb coldness, setting it afire. He wanted to charge at them, to kill them with his bare hands. Yet he could barely stand straight.

"I reckon it's only human," Younts drawled to Terrebine, "for a man to blame somebody else for his own weaknesses."

"Don't ever think you've beaten me!" Ragan gasped. "Don't think it for a minute!"

Terrebine stiffened at the rasping of that voice. "Pay the man off, Angel," he said coldly. "I kept my promise. But he can't hold down a man-sized job."

"The hell with your money," Ragan breathed. "When I collect from you two, you'll pay through the nose." Aggressive, boiling for action, but helpless, he walked out.

The white stallion was still in the trap, had not yet quieted down. As Ragan reeled across the ranchyard, it whipped about the corral, rearing and whistling, its scream terrifying to hear. Going on to the regular day corral, Ragan managed to snake out the horse he had borrowed from Pace Hanna. Somehow he got the saddle cinched on its back. Nobody offered to help him, or even showed himself in the yard.

He rode for Ladder and what he knew would now be the

one, dedicated purpose of his life. The decision was final, adamant. He was still working right.

Pace was still out on the roundup with Spade. It was Nancy who saw the rider come into the yard, swaying in the saddle. She saw the sweat-plastered face, the streaks of blood under nostrils and lips. Above all, she saw the wildness of Ragan's staring eyes.

"Chance—what happened?" she cried and ran to him.

Seeing her, hearing the deep concern in her husky voice, Ragan was steadied a little. He slid out of the saddle and was no longer too proud to let her catch a part of his weight and support it on her shoulders. A man had need of a woman's tenderness in a rough and hostile world.

"They think they beat me, Nancy!" he panted. "But they never! And, by God, they never will!" He had to tell her that, to make her see the real Ragan that nothing would ever subdue.

"Of course not! But what was it?"

"Younts—Terrebine—at Fork. They had an outlaw stallion and goaded me into forking it. Nearly had it beat. Then my bum leg let go. It threw me—pretty hard."

"Why, the dirty devils!"

They had reached the house porch, where he dropped into an old rocking chair. He leaned back, shutting his eyes, feeling everything whirling again. Pretty soon he felt pressure against his teeth.

Nancy said, "Take a pull on this."

It was whiskey. He drew in a gulp, then another, and felt the liquid hit his battered stomach and burn. It nauseated him, but he managed to hold it down.

"Chance, you only tackled too much too soon."

"Nothin' can beat me—nothin', Nancy."

"I've never been surer of anything in all my life."

He stared up at her with dull eyes. "You mean that?"

"I sure do."

"Thanks."

He felt better. Out of the whole John Day only Pace and Nancy believed that nothing had changed. But their faith was solid, worth more than his own life. He felt her hand on the skin of his neck. Something flowed from her and entered him, a part of her abundant strength. It helped settle the wildness of his mind and emotions; it made him feel alive again.

51

"Chance, for me will you lie down and rest a while?" she asked.

"All right," he agreed, vividly aware in that moment of her yellow hair, the deep brown of her eyes, the warm, human sympathy of her face. He had need of those things—he needed them dreadfully.

He followed her into the house, then stretched out on the bed they had given him to use. He lay in a half stupor, but the whiskey she had given him had a relaxing effect so he could at least lie still. He could keep from thinking, almost from feeling, finally. At last he drifted off.

He awakened to find that Nancy had put a blanket over him, that night had come. He rose to a sit on the bed and found that the dizziness had left him. Standing, he felt sore in every muscle and joint, but his insides no longer hurt him.

Even as he reached for the boots Nancy must have taken off him, she appeared in the doorway, highlighted by the lamp in the other room. She said, "Oh, you're awake. Judd Kildane's here and wants to see you. I refused to wake you up."

"Judd? What could he want of me?"

"He says it's important."

She went out, and Ragan finished pulling on his boots. He settled his feet in them and went outside. Judd had waited in the yard, but the light from the doorway illuminated the look on his face, uneasy and uncertain. The long, lean body was tense.

He said, "Chance, you're going to guess it, anyhow, so I'll speak out. Joy made me come over here to see you." He waited an instant, and when Ragan only shrugged said, "She told me she'd tried to interest you in a business proposition. It looks like she's pretty set on it, even yet."

"And whaever it is," said Ragan, "you don't like it, do you?"

Judd shrugged. "Joy's her own boss, with her own money. If she wants to back you, I figure it's her business."

"You know she's trying to build me into her idea of a husband."

"Don't see how you figure that's so bad," Judd said tartly. "Look at her side of it. Could she marry some cowpoke, after the raising she had, and be happy with it? Or could she marry one and make him a present of her half of Teeter? From what she's told me, she only wants to loan you money and let you take it from there. I figure that's a

52

compliment to you. And a hell of a lot more than she'd do for any other man."

"All right," Ragan snapped. "Now you can go home and tell her you tried. The same as Arch tried to give me a job because she wanted him to."

"Glad to," Judd said angrily, and strode toward his horse. Like Terrebine, he had gone through the pretense of humoring Joy.

Ragan watched the receding man for a long while. He knew how it had bent Judd's pride to come over and make that kind of talk. It could have happened only because Joy had kept pushing him. That meant her desire to resume the old relationship was persistent and real. And she offered a way to fight Terrebine at his own level.

Where a day ago Ragan had scorned the thought of such help, he now found it tempting. His smoldering resentment had been whipped into flame by what had happened at Fork. Terrebine had his secret backer. There was no reason, beyond pride, why Ragan should not have one. Yet pride made him yearn to triumph in the ways they considered impossible to him.

Turning then, he saw Nancy standing on the porch, the sun bright on her yellow head. He didn't know how much she had heard of what had passed between him and Judd.

She only smiled and said, "Breakfast's ready, Chance."

Noting the expression on her face, Ragan knew he would stick with the three who had proved themselves once and forever, who would always believe in him, no matter what.

Nancy rode up to Squabble Creek with him the next morning. It was mainly to lend him company, for he was already familiar with the place. Except for its command of one of the passes to Auburn and Sparta, there was nothing to distinguish it. The setting was a large, flat-bottomed valley like a hundred others in the tangled Blues.

The line camp's log dugout sat under the north bench. Water churned out of a spring for the use of the house and corrals, while Squabble Creek carried water from one end of the flat to the other before losing itself in the hills. There was a fenced horse pasture west of the structures. On the terrace above the bench grew yellow pine. All about the flat ran interconnecting plateaus, most of which lay behind Spade, Ladder and Teeter, and thus were assigned to those ranches by common consent of the cow country.

The Squabble Creek camp had once been a small independent cattle operation and thus was more complete than the usual line camp. Ragan walked about with Nancy, looking over the log barn with its attached shed, the several pole corrals, the stacker-pole where somebody had once put up hay. Springfed cottonwood screened the dugout, but by climbing the talus behind, a man could sweep the whole flat.

Ragan looked at these things, and thought: this is it—my starting point. There were wrongs to be righted, losses to regain. Afterward he could look ahead, to a home and wife and family, to the goodness of life after so much of its bitterness, despair and hate which were not native in Chance Ragan.

Before she left for home, Nancy said, "You eat and get some weight on you, Chance. And don't brood over what idiots have done to you. Would you do that much for a towheaded kid?"

He had to laugh at her. She liked hearing the sound come out of him and joined in. It was odd that he had never noticed before that a dimple appeared on her tanned cheek when she was amused. Then he watched her ride out for Ladder, a straight and easy figure in the leather.

He remained in front of the dugout and smoked a cigarette, just looking around. Kitch had not stretched things a bit when he spoke of the repair work the place needed. A summer and winter camp were two different things entirely. Before the snow flew, and the cold winds began to howl across the mountains, the roofs had to be patched and the walls chinked. The fences needed work, the shack could use more furniture and shelving, there was stove wood to lay up in plenty. Finally there would be the cattle that would arrive as soon as roundup was finished. He had got back a place in the world. It was meager, maybe laughable to a Kildane, but for the moment he was satisfied.

He still had the roan he had borrowed from Pace, and he spent the rest of that day in the saddle. He had been through the flat a number of times in his days as a cattle dealer, but now wanted to familiarize himself with it intimately. In addition, he wanted to spend as much time on leather as he could manage. He was going to make his body tough, strong and hard again, as invulnerable as was the secret spirit so deep in his being. The prospect of doing that successfully kept excitement running in him.

He put in a second day doing nothing but riding. When

54

he knew every landmark, every pitfall for cattle, every game trail for his own use and every other characteristic of the vicinity, he took an axe and rode to the timber to fell poles. They would be the rough material for firewood and fence posts and repairs to the buildings as he needed them.

Beyond that, the chopping was the kind of hard, muscular toil he craved. For several days more he worked steadily from daylight until dark. The work made him eat heartily and sleep through the nights. Frequently when he shaved off his accumulation of whiskers, the mirror told him he was picking up fast.

I told them, he thought gleefully. I told the sons-of-bitches.

Riding down one day for his noon meal, he topped the high terrace to see a saddled horse standing in the yard below him. He didn't recognize the animal and supposed it was somebody from Spade or Ladder come up to check on him. But when he had dropped down and rode closer he drew up in surprise. The horse wore the brand of Kildane's Teeter. He looked thoughtful as he rode on into the yard.

A figure appeared in the dugout doorway, slender and lithe. Joy said, "I was beginning to wonder if you never got hungry, Chance."

Ragan could only sit the saddle and feel the hard thump of his heart. He was hungry indeed. This utter aloneness with her, and the increasing vitality of his body, made that plainer than at any time since his return to the range. Hungry for the slim, perfect body of this woman, even when his mind disapproved of her views. He had hoped that this would grow less, yet as he became more of a man again it had grown stronger.

He did not like that, yet did not deny the truth of it. She knew she had her hold on him and meant to use it.

She wore a special smile for him as she waited. It was a gesture of friendship, for the last time they parted she had been angry. Her reason for temper had increased when he had turned Judd down so summarily that evening at Ladder. Ragan let his gaze slide down to her left hand, held at the front of a supple thigh. There was no ring there yet.

She knew what he had looked for, and her expression changed. The smile quit her, and uncertainty tugged down the corners of her mouth. Then the smile returned.

"That's right," she said. "I die hard, I guess. You and I are alike in one thing, anyhow. We won't let ourselves be

55

licked. But don't let me scare you. I didn't come up to fight some more. Only to make peace."

He swung down, hoping she saw how easily he did it.

"Then welcome, and let's eat," he answered.

"Thank you," Joy said, relieved.

Ragan did the cooking, unapologetic for the crude facilities he had to offer her. They could talk lightly again, referring to nothing that was very important, Ragan wanting to ask the questions that squirmed in his mind.

One was how she had known she could find him here. That could be important. If he was being watched as closely as it indicated, Terrebine and Younts might realize, already, that his main purpose in being here was to spy on their covert activities.

He decided he had better put that one to her and said, "How'd you track me down?"

"Through grapevine rumor," she said lightly. "I saw Eudora Parker in Long Creek. She goes with a Spade puncher. He'd told her Kitch is making up a herd to winter up here. Putting two and two together, I knew where to find you. Wish I hadn't?"

He wasn't quick to reassure her. Thoughtfully he said, "Joy, when you can come to a man just because you want him, mebbe you and me can do business. But I can't stand being built up to suit you. I don't aim to, ever."

He saw her breath run in quickly and hold a second in her perfect breast. Then, "I know we need to start over, Chance. I've been too candid, but that's how I'm built. I could have pretended to be something different and have fooled you, probably. Then set out to manage you cunningly. A lot of women do that, but I won't. I'm not high-minded, and I know it. I'm ambitious. I'm passionate. Whether or not it shocks you, I want to sleep with you. But not enough so I'd consider the world well lost for love."

"I do like your honesty."

"What don't you like?"

"I still think you're doing more scheming than you let on."

She raised her head quickly, then smiled. "I'm not going to get angry at your bluntness any more. That's your way of being honest, too. It's the best footing for us, Chance, from here on."

"There'll be a from here on?"

"If I can possibly manage one. And that, my friend, is the extent of my scheming. I like your refusal to be de-

56

feated. I'm going to be likewise. But let's eat before you let everything burn up."

He laughed, and that was as far as personal matters progressed with them. They ate, talking over valley news and news from the outside world that had drifted in. Then Joy mounted her horse and rode out.

She left Ragan stirred and puzzled. He knew her well enough to suspect she had had a more definite motive in coming than she had admitted. Maybe it had only been to re-impress her exquisite self on his senses. If so, she had succeeded tenfold. Again she was a flaming image in his brain, a hunger in all his healing body. And she wanted him that way, too.

8

THE TIME drew near for the cattle to arrive from Spade and Ladder. Ragan set to work against winter in dead earnest, knowing the fierceness of the storms that could roar over the Blues with little warning. He cut wood and chinked walls and patched roofs, getting the buildings tight. He fixed fences, cleaned out the springs and dug the earth tanks bigger. He could feel his roots sinking into the earth of Squabble Flat, his gaunt body thriving from the strength they drew.

Meanwhile he watched the flat and its trails, but saw nothing more of Younts or any Fork rider. He worried about their suspecting his main reason for being up here. Yet, from what he knew of their illegal operations, he believed the flat was a vital link for them. They would have to use it, whether or not they were on guard against his spying.

That, or they would have to remove him from the flat in a way that could not be traced to them. There was only one way to do that—another and successful try at murder.

Deeper than these considerations, and a mounting relief to him, was the weight he put on steadily. It didn't come all at once, the flesh and stamina and sense of well-being that meant a body in good shape. But his hands, shriveled and stiffened by the freezing, had now turned brown and calloused. The foot and leg that had been wasted and weakened lent themselves better to his use. Sometimes he would seem to hear music and see couples dancing, himself among them.

When he had a woodpile that satisfied him, he banked more dirt against the walls of the dugout, knowing how much it would increase the warmth inside. He fixed himself a couple more shelves and braced the wobbly old chairs. He replaced the bunk and cut new grass to pad it. He became aware of loneliness and grew impatient for the coming of the cattle.

They still had not arrived, although he was ready for them and the rigors of wintering them out. Having nothing left to do at the camp, he decided to ride down to the valley to see what was holding things up. Perhaps he could bring the winter herd up himself, if they were just short of help.

He rode in early that day for his supper, intending to go down to Spade that evening and spend the night. He turned his horse into the corral and started for the dugout. He was only a few steps from its sunken doorway when something whipped past him, seeming almost to touch his cheek.

Up on the bench behind the dugout, a rifle cracked viciously.

He could only bolt on toward the dugout in lunging strides. He was nearly there when his awkward foot tangled and he went sprawling headlong. Again he heard the wicked crack of the weapon, up above somewhere. This time the bullet gouged into the earth close to his head. He crawled hastily on and rolled down the dugout steps. In bitter impotence he cursed the leg for its betrayal of him in a pinch. Then he began to think of the attacker, and will-power rushed into him, instant and unyielding.

His shell belt hung on a peg driven into the inside wall, next to the dugout door. Entering the place, he took it down, his nerves still flinching but his mind again stable and cool. He buckled on the belt and stepped once more to the door.

Due to the angle at which the building set against the cliff, he could move back outdoors without danger. When he had done so, he halted, pressed tight against the wall. He could hear nothing but the breeze moving over the flat. By cutting sharply to the right, he worked himself safely into the brush, then on past the spring. He stopped there a moment, like a rooted plant, his eyes coldly searching through the screen of brush.

He saw no tattling sign of movement on the rimrock but felt certain the rifleman was still up there. He was dead sure as to who had sent him here on a killer's mission. This awareness keened his mind and senses, whetted his hungers. He wanted that fellow. If he waited long enough, the man would move. Ragan had patience. He'd had to practice it a lot in recent months.

Still nothing showed on the sharp line of the bluff lip. Then, at long last, the waiting paid off. The fellow had shifted himself a little farther away from Ragan. He sought a better angle to the dugout, where he believed his man still to be. Ragan saw the barrel of the rifle for a second, a short sharp glint in the sun.

He went on, moving away from the man because he knew how to climb onto the rim from a point a little farther south. At the end of the spring's copse he bellied across to the rock and dirt of the talus. The movement was not contested. Presently he dared to rise to a crouch so he could climb. He moved up through the rocks and at last lifted himself over the bench.

The roughness of the top cut him from sight of the killer. He pulled off his boots. Afterward he circled until he was directly behind the man's position. Then he started in toward the lip again, never hesitating. Soundlessly he came up over the swell, which gave him a dead shot at the killer.

He didn't shoot, instead yelled out as he loomed there, aggressive, menacing.

"Lift your arms, buck!"

He was grimly, angrily amused at what the surprise did to the man's nerves. The killer clawed around, swinging the rifle. He spotted Ragan and found himself looking into the muzzle of a Colt .45. Rage, fear, then panic tangled on his face so that he did nothing whatsoever.

"Take it easy, Squint," Ragan warned. "It's a long fall if I blast you over the edge."

Squint Lister had a Winchester .30-30, but he let go of it then. He stayed there on his knees. His mouth had sagged open, and he raised his arms up finally. His hooded eyelids had pulled wide.

"So now you're trying for outright murder," Ragan rapped. "You boys sure change your system. Younts could have let me get killed by a horse but didn't. Now you're trying to bushwhack me. How come?"

Lister waited in open worry, expecting to receive the treatment he would himself have administered. He breathed, "Man, you've proved yourself tougher than anybody figured you could be."

"Than who figured? Younts, Terrebine or you?"

"It looks like this is between you and me, don't it?"

"Where's your horse?" Ragan demanded. "I'm taking you back to Fork. It's your say whether that's dead or alive."

Lister thought a moment, then pointed. "The cayuse is down in the bottom at the end of the bench."

"We'll get him. Start walking, man." The beating words pushed at the killer; they turned him uncertain and at last defeated him.

Driving Lister ahead of him, Ragan went back to where he had left his boots. He made the disarmed man stand at a safe distance while he got the footgear on again. Then they dropped down to the flat, where Lister's mount was hidden in the brush.

Ragan led the horse as they circled the brush and returned to the dugout. There he made Lister resaddle the roan. Presently they were mounted and riding for Younts' backhills ranch.

It was something that Ragan burned to do, although he knew how dangerous it was for him. Once more he had beaten Younts, as he had on the cattle drive to Dixie. The fact restored much of his self-confidence, maybe made him reckless, too. He didn't care about that right now.

Dusk was thick about them when they came in sight of Fork. Riding on into the ranchyard, Ragan saw a man come to the open door of the bunkhouse and look out, the lamplight bright on his figure.

"Stub," Ragan rapped, "get Younts out here. I want to see the bastard."

The man stepped back. Beyond the windows figures stirred in sudden energy. Then Younts appeared in the doorway, hatless, the light glistening on his head. He saw the cowed Lister, the gun in Ragan's hand. For a moment he stood still and quiet.

Then he said, "Well, I'll be damned," and again fell silent.

"That's the third time you've tried it," Ragan breathed. "The first I never had a chance. The second I could have killed the cheap gunmen you sent to get me. I could have killed this coyote and that has used up your free chances, Angel. From here on I kill on sight."

Bluster came up in the hairless Younts. He straightened his square body and stared out at Ragan. The emotions that swirled in him turned him reckless.

"All right," he answered heavily. "You got no pride. A man can make a fool of you, but you keep dogging on."

"If you'd realized that, you'd have let the stud kill me, would you?"

"I reckon we made a mistake there," Younts admitted. "We thought you'd drag your freight."

"I won't ever leave this country with my tail between my legs," Ragan said fiercely. "You seem to realize that, finally. But don't send any more killers after me, Angel, if you want to see 'em alive again."

Abruptly he swung his horse and rode out, a stubborn man whose crashing defiance left uneasy men behind him.

He was glad he had done the thing for the sake of his pride. Yet he realized he had pitted himself openly against men who would soon brush aside his warning. He headed back to Squabble Creek, because a hunch had come to him. Noting the flat and its relation to the upper mountains, something had connected in his mind. He wanted to do some more investigating immediately.

The night passed peacefully. The next morning he ate a quick breakfast, saddled the roan and rode out, striking due eastward over the flat. The divide that let riders and cattle across the Blues had thrown his thinking off until now. The pass itself might not mean a thing in the rustling operations. What interested him now was the wild country running directly behind Fork, Younts' own ranch, on this side of the mountains and south of the divide.

It was clear that Younts did his rustling in the winter, exploiting the long interval between calf roundups. Now Ragan wondered if the country back of the man's layout might not disclose a place where stolen cattle could be held for long periods, to be let down as needed into Fork's corrals. It might connect with or even be the mountain hideout he had himself discovered, in remote country not familiar to him.

If that was the case, Squabble Flat would have to be crossed side to side, instead of traveled lengthwise by the stolen cattle. Denied the ability to cross it, the rustlers would be completely obstructed. That explained why Younts had passed up the chance to let the stallion kill him in the guise of an accident. He had thought that shame would run him out of the country. Then, when Ragan had shown up at this vital point, Younts had seen his error and sent Squint Lister with his rifle.

In so doing, Younts had tipped the balances in Ragan's mind

61

as to what was really going on. Thereby he might have made yet another mistake.

The air was crisp enough to chill Ragan as he rode, bearing a strengthened hint of the winter close at hand. Crossing the sage flat, he began to ride studiously along the south edge, where the uplifts broke above him. He knew that what he searched for would not be big and glaring but an unobtrusive opening into the primitive area.

He passed a place before it nagged at his interest enough to turn him around and take him back. There was nothing to see, though, but another crease in the crinkled hills, like a dozen others ahead of him and behind. Rain and freezing ground had long since buried any significant tracks of cattle. But old droppings lay in the gully to an extent worth investigating.

He turned the horse into the draw and began to pick his way forward at a walk. For a while he followed the brown, twisting wrinkle through the hills without much interest. Then he came to a dry wash he had not observed on his previous exploring. He stood the horse there to study the bed of the wash. He recognized it as one of the many small channels that ran water in winter while going dry in the summertime.

He saw what use could be made of it, and was convinced that he followed a rewarding line of thought. Below the loose banks of the watercourse, the water line showed that it never achieved much depth. Winter-rustled steers could be driven along its course for any distance without leaving a detectable trail.

This was what he had hoped to find, his basis for conclusive action.

Still reined in, he folded his hands on the saddlehorn and considered how he would use the stream if Squabble Flat were vacated for the winter. If rustled in stormy weather, cattle could be drifted onto the flat without much danger of being discovered. Rain or new snow would wipe out the tracks in short order. Later, cuts could be pushed on through this channel to a more permanent concealment in the hinterland. He had found one such place himself. From there they could go down to Younts' corrals. He grinned in rising excitement and rode on.

He climbed slowly with the watercourse, the notch of the draw widening while the onward hills grew high. As he pierced deeper into the wasteland, he began to question his theory. Then all at once he topped out onto another of the country's many high flats. This one was narrow, not long. A brushy dry creek ran down its center line. The watershed of this section, he knew, caused the dry wash he had followed.

Again he found copious droppings. This particular coulee was too small to accommodate many steers and was not the place he had seen before. He rode on toward the brush-closed end of the flat, where the mountain notch began again beyond. Soon he noticed a strange thing about the brush clump that concealed the lower part of the notch.

It seemed to be dead along its whole length. The brook bed narrowed and flattened out, and he saw a boulder field just short of the brush patch. He lifted his horse to a trot, swung wide of the boulders, then turned back in. The brush was dead, indeed, and for good cause. It had no roots. It was a brush fence erected for a double purpose—concealment as well as obstruction.

He had all the proof he needed to confirm his theory.

At this point, above the head of the little stream, he was too low to see past the brush fence. He was wary now, although the chances were against anybody's being here at the moment. The fence had taken work and care and was over three hundred feet long. He found the gate at the west end, a section that could be lifted out. It was too heavy for him to raise and, stepping down from the saddle, he made his way around the end of the fence afoot and went on.

The gully continued. His sense of expectancy was high, and he soon found that it was justified. A hundred yards farther on, he came to a much larger flat, one big enough to do the job he knew had been assigned to it.

His viewpoint was different, and there were no cattle in sight now, but he realized it was the place he had discovered after his camp had been shot up. Younts had moved the cattle out, at least temporarily, in fear that he would send or bring in the law.

He still was not sure of his exact location. He would have liked to explore this section, also, and see what it connected with farther south. But he had crowded his luck in coming here at all, and there was another angle he had to investigate. Returning to his horse, he stepped up to the saddle and rode back the way he had come.

When he reached the place where he had first come upon the wash, riding in from Squabble Creek, he stayed in the dry watercourse and kept on, following it downward. He was curious as to whether the winter waterflow was used to bring steers in or to take them out again. He wanted to see where the dry bed came out into the lower, grazing country.

He had his answer within the hour, for he found himself all at once dropped down onto Wildcat Creek where it entered Younts' range. You've got it nailed down, he told himself, except that there isn't a steer up there right now. You can't do anything more till they've moved again themselves.

He was sobered by the proved fact that he had placed himself squarely athwart the plans of Terrebine and Younts. They were rustling only in bad weather and did not risk taking stolen stuff directly from its home range to Younts' holding pens. So they probably were not taking it into the hideout hole the same way it came out again. That would put the stuff too close to Younts' spread. So Squabble Creek Flat was indispensable to their activities. It was bound to see fighting before long.

Looking about, he wondered how best to get home without running into immediate trouble. If he stuck with Wildcat Creek, he would come eventually to Spade. That caused him to remember his previous intention of visiting Kitch Dunsan, maybe to take up the winter cattle himself. He was considering that visit again when, all at once, he heard horses coming in the distance. They approached from the direction of Fork.

He moved without thinking, not wanting to be seen. The quickest way back to Squabble Creek was the route he had used coming down, along the dry wash. He whipped his horse into it, laying tracks as visible as red lanterns. He dismissed that now, for he had already marked the wash with sign from end to end. He knew at once that they had heard him and speeded their horses in pursuit.

But it was country that offered no hiding place, and he trusted the roan's ability to stay ahead. He leaned forward, urging the horse on at its top gait. When, a little later, he pulled down, he could hear nothing behind him. But he pressed on, considering how to get home without leading them there behind him.

Five minutes later he reined in again to let his ears keen for sound. There still was none of the kind he listened for. They apparently had given up the chase. He spurred his tiring horse, after that, still riding steadily but at a more moderate speed.

Then, for the third time, he halted to listen and heard the

faint sound of drumming hoofs again, well in the rearward distance. He still conserved his horse, although now he rode a little faster. Then, without warning, he rounded a turn in the draw to find a horse squarely blocking him. The rider held a carbine, and it was leveled at him.

"Gettin' yourself an eyeful?" rapped Squint Lister. The hoods of his eyes were pulled tight.

"Where in hell did you come from?" Ragan gasped.

Lister laughed, and it was an ugly sound of warning. His eyes were streaked with the hostility wrought by his humiliation the day before.

He said, "You ain't learned all the byways yet, Ragan. Stub kept in the wash to occupy that busy mind of your'n while I cut straight for the flat and turned back in ahead of you. Ought to have got more schooling in it, man, before you turned range detective. It's gonna cost you what you wiggled out of yesterday."

Ragan stiffened in the saddle, not lifting his hands. In the quiet he could hear the rearward rider, who had fooled and driven him into this trap.

"You're getting things figured out," Squint was saying. "But you just ain't bright enough to take a fair warning. Now, you hold up your arms while I ride over and take that hogleg."

Fear turned in Ragan then. Men like Squint, like Younts, knew many ways of killing without arousing provable suspicions in the decent gentry. The threat in the man's eyes now was bald, chilling.

Stalling for time, searching for a way out of this, Ragan said, "I got the idea your try yesterday was only a scare shot. You sure Younts wants me beefed now, Squint?"

"Yesterday it was different. After you left Fork, Angel said we'd take take care of you the first chance. I got the chance, right now."

"Figure it'll square you for looking like a idiot yesterday, do you?"

"It'll square me good."

Squint sidled his horse over, while Ragan weighed his chances. They were not good, yet would get no better. He knew Lister would shoot him if he made the slightest hostile move. But the man's carbine was more awkward at close quarters than a hand gun would be. Ragan knew he had to risk it. After Stub Nelson came up, there would be no chance at all.

Lister moved in cautiously. He was kneeing his horse,

65

which hesitated about coming so close to the other animal. He would have his hands full in that instant when he reached over to take Ragan's pistol, not having trusted his captive to draw and hand it over. Ragan began to lower an upraised hand toward the brim of his hat.

As Squint's wary features moved close to him, he jerked off the hat and used it to swipe the man hard across the eyes. His other hand hit the carbine barrel and deflected it as it cracked out with a shot. He locked onto Squint desperately, the two horses wheeling apart. The men fell together to the ground.

Ragan was on top, still holding onto the carbine with his left hand. He used the other hand to try to free his revolver, but he couldn't get it loose from under his body. Cursing wildly, Squint tried to wrestle him off. They writhed and rolled through ugly seconds on the hot sand of the dry wash. Ragan dared not think of the other Fork rider coming on from below. This was life or death, with that a separate crisis if he managed to survive this.

Squint had an arm around his neck, was trying to use it to shut off his wind. The man stood a chance to lose a second time, and the prospect gave him the strength of desperation. Yet he had only to hold on until Stub came up. Ragan discerned that intention, and his urgency gave him a kind of detachment of mind. He rolled himself slightly, taking his weight off his .45. But he still lay on it, and Squint's body kept him from turning enough to free the gun.

He used his head to butt Squint's sweating, hate-twisted face. The man held on stoically, waiting for help to arrive. He guessed Ragan's intentions and rolled himself harder to his right, farther burying the covered pistol. Ragan rested a moment, his breath pumping through his open mouth. He caught the still distant racket of the oncoming horse and felt panic. The hospital months hadn't been good training for this, the work afterward hadn't done quite enough. Fatigue was a sick weight in his muscles.

To free his gun he had to roll over on top of Squint. The man knew what he wanted to do and was bending his full strength to prevent it. Ragan quit butting and all at once sank his teeth into the base of Squint's neck. The man yelled and loosened the arm he had around Ragan's head. Ragan used the seconds lent him by that to heave himself on top. He tried again to free his gun.

He got the grips, but his weight was still on the barrel.

66

He rolled on over and, as he did so, lost his hold on Squint's carbine. Ragan rolled clear free, scrambling up. As he got to his knees, he saw that Squint had flapped over with the carbine, was jacking the lever as he raised up. Ragan's hand streaked for his .45. Squint held the carbine stock against his side and used his body to aim. His mouth opened in its gasping, and his slitted eyes were wild.

Ragan brought up his gun, having no choice. He shot and threw himself aside as he heard the carbine's spiteful crack. But Squint had gone over backward, the carbine lifting with him then, released, thrown on over his head. Ragan's mind was racing as he staggered to his feet. The approaching horse apparently had been stopped when its rider heard the shooting. That was a break, for if Stub came on he would do so warily. Ragan paused only long enough to take a look at Squint.

He had shot the man through the chest, and Squint was dead already. Ragan got his hat and started on up the wash at a lurching run. Around the next turn, he saw his own horse in the forward distance. It had bolted, then, showing its training, had halted. Ragan went toward it in long, uneven strides.

Behind a distant voice was bawling, "Hey, Squint—!"

Ragan reached the horse and mounted, bent only on getting away. Stub would come on carefully to the place where the fight had occurred. What he would find there would hold him a while, and Ragan doubted that the man would come on after him single-handed. Ragan swung the roan around and roweled it on along the wash.

9

AFTER FIVE minutes, Ragan halted and could hear nothing behind him. When he came to the turn-off defile that could take him out to Squabble Flat, his lank body began to throw off its tenseness. He spilled out onto the home flat, long later, only to pull down his horse in surprise.

Cattle dotted the expanse ahead of him, and he knew the winter stuff had been brought in while he was away. At another time this would have pleased him, for he had wanted steers about him, a puncher's full work to do. He struck out to the creek, then turned down toward the distant headquarters. It was past noon, he realized, and he had been in the saddle since early morning. Physically he again felt strong and good. He had fought a sound man and beaten him, and his mind ran instantly to the tougher fights ahead.

His sense of triumph over what he had just achieved soon turned to doubt. He had no regret for having killed Lister, for that had been essential to his survival. But the manner in which it had happened began to worry him. He had killed and run away because he had been obliged to flee. Now, with more detachment, he was concerned about what Younts might make of that escape.

He saw only one horse at the line camp. As he rode closer, his mouth broke into a tired grin. A girl stood in the yard watching him. He recognized Nancy as he rode on, his sudden depression lifting when he saw her genial smile. It struck him how good it was to have a woman waiting for him. He touched his hat and swung down beside her, watching her tanned face change to a look of surprise when she saw his torn and dirty clothing. Her dimple vanished. Its going was like a cloud across the sun.

"What on earth happened to you this time?" she gasped.

He didn't want to tell anybody about Lister until he had had time to think it over. "I strayed off my range," he said, "and a gent objected. But we got it straightened out. Forget it."

"Did you learn something, Chance?"

"Only that Pace and Kitch are dead right in what they think about Younts and Terrebine." Then, because he wanted to change the subject, "You didn't bring the steers up by yourself, did you?"

Nancy shook her yellow head. "Slim Gallatin helped, but he didn't have time to hang around and wait for you. Dad and Kitch are pushing the beef cut to Baker City. They said they'll send up horses and feed as soon as they get home."

Knowing she disapproved of him in some ways, he had a sudden deep wish to please her.

"Speaking of feed, let's put on the nosebag ourselves," he said, smiling at her.

"Suits me to a T." The dimple came back again.

She wore waist overalls and a boy's plaid shirt. Her hair was caught under her hat, and her long-legged slimness attracted him. He remembered her quick affinity for Kitch and wondered again what their plans were. But Nancy would

68

have no trouble finding a husband when she was ready; she could take her pick of the country's best. Noticing his secret interest in her girlish body, she flushed and walked down into the dugout.

He wondered if she ever wanted a man, the way Joy had confessed so frankly.

He watered the roan, unsaddled and turned it into the pasture. The string of mounts promised him would probably come up next, and he had a puncher's desire for plenty of horseflesh. Again he felt regret at what had happened in the hills. He was getting what he wanted here, and the other disturbed and endangered his peace of mind, even if nothing worse came of it.

He ought to ride to Canyon City and tell the sheriff the whole story. But that would end the hope of catching the rustlers in a way that would make their conviction certain. That aspect of the situation was more important than his own serenity. Cattlemen far and wide were losing steers, being bled white, with only a couple of them so much as suspecting it. He had become the key piece in a matter of gigantic importance, was obliged to accept what came of it. Quickly, like the whole man he had once been, his mind was firmed.

Nancy had started a fire by the time Ragan reached the dugout. She said, "If I'd had an idea when you'd be back, I'd have had dinner waiting. What'll it be?"

She dimpled again, and he laughed because that was a senseless question on a cattle ranch. She had already opened a can of beans. There would be bacon and coffee, and frying pan bread if she felt ambitious. Ragan told her to handle the cooking department and seated himself comfortably. As he pulled out tobacco, he realized how steady his hands had become. He no longer had to hold his shriveled leg out straight to stop its aching.

Reversing his worry, he again savored the fact that he had been locked in a life-or-death struggle with a vicious killer and had come off best. He made a cigarette with swift, even movements, watching Nancy go busily about her work. She fit in with his way of life, a fact that she took for granted.

"You've sure fixed the place up nice," she commented.

"Figure on sending for a mail-order wife."

She looked at him quickly but said nothing. In the softened light of the dugout, he noticed, her hair and skin were almost the same color.

He considered telling her about Lister, in order to have

69

somebody who could talk on his side of the argument if one came up. Yet that would do little good, he realized. She had witnessed neither the chase nor the fight. Moreover, what he could tell her, at this point, might be dangerous to her, with her father away on the cattle drive. He decided again to keep the matter to himself.

When Nancy had food on the table, they sat down to eat together. A little rested now, Ragan felt even better. Nancy, whose spirits were always bouyant, chatted while she ate, telling him the latest news from the lower country. There was nothing of importance; it was just the kind of talk the cow country liked to pass around whenever two people got together.

Then she surprised him by turning serious all at once, saying, "Chance, why have you stuck off up here by yourself, with no stock to pin you down? We'd like to see you once in a while. And they're still having dances at Cottonwood every Saturday night."

Ragan felt a flush climb into his face because he had sensed this secret censure in her. "Well, I've been busy without any livestock. See that woodpile out there? The new sections in the fences? The holes I patched in the roof? I done all that in addition to prettying up the dugout."

Some unswerving purpose kept her eyes on him steadily, her clear, young face unchanging.

"Just the same, Chance, you've turned bunch quitter."

He frowned. The accusation didn't anger him, the way he had been aroused when Younts called him a cut-back. A bunch quitter was a different breed of critter, an animal that refused to run with its kind, and kept to itself. Maybe she was right about him turning into one. He didn't know except that he no longer had a desire to do the things she suggested. He had grown to like being alone, to work at his obsessive purpose of bringing back the old Ragan. That took time, persistence, and left no room for frivolities. She didn't understand such things and suddenly he felt twice her age.

"It's not that," he said doubtfully. "At least, I don't think so. I kind of went on a drunk up here, you might say. Doing the things I couldn't do for so long. Things I didn't know if I'd ever be doing again. I am doing 'em. That seems to be all I want." He wished she would drop it. She was making him conscious of his skinny weaknesses again.

"I know. I saw the woodpile and all the rest. Kitch is

70

more than getting his money's worth out of this. You're getting back on your feet. But that's not enough."

Determined to change the subject, he said, "I riled you the time I called Kitch a fuzz-cheek, didn't I?"

"Why not? It was the same as calling me unweaned, too."

He looked at her closely. He hadn't realized that he had belittled her at the same time. He laughed, saying, "You're grown, all right. No doubt of that." His breath caught with some sudden excitement when she flushed.

"I'm glad you realize it at last," she said tartly. "But you aren't throwing me off the track. I wish you'd come down and mix with people once in a while, the way you used to."

"If you want it, then I will."

"That's a promise I'll hold you to," she said doubtfully.

"All right," he agreed. "Anything to please the nicest yellow-head on Wildcat Creek." His smile warmed the coolness out of her.

She helped him wash up the dishes, then left for Ladder. Ragan watched her ride out straight and slender in the saddle, while something changed in him again. The fight was taking its toll, at last, of a body not really mended. His bones ached, his nerves had turned back on edge, and there was a feeling of revulsion in him. She hadn't meant to do it, but she had helped stir that up in him.

But it made one thing clear. He had more work to do before he was the man he wanted to be again. Meanwhile, he had no time for anything else. Afterward—but would there be any afterward? He was locked in the fight of his life. Like the tumblers of a lock, his mind closed again on that purpose.

Work was still the answer to his problem, and he had plenty of it now to do. The herd, nearly three hundred head of shorthorns, would have to be watched closely until it had settled itself here. So he saddled up the next morning and rode around the flat, throwing back such critters as had poked off into the defiles of the hills. This gave him little trouble. Fall grass had started, and the main bunch was content to keep to the flat and its handy water.

He had barely got back to headquarters when Slim Gallatin came in, leading four strung-out horses. Spade had furnished them and had not worked off any of its sorry critters on him. Gallatin was gawky, a good-natured man who had ridden for Spade for years. He stayed to have the noon meal with Ragan, then struck out for home.

It puzzled Ragan when several days passed without a visit

71

from the sheriff about Squint Lister. Younts wouldn't dare conceal the death of even a hardcase, although he would not be anxious to invite the law in here. Ragan began to wonder if Lister had pulled through, as some of that tough breed could. His decision firmed anew. He would sit tight on that matter as long as Younts did.

Meanwhile he worked faithfully with his cattle and horses and once more felt strength building back into his body. He remembered his promise to Nancy. No matter how he felt about it, he ought to humor her. But he wouldn't go down for a visit yet. Certainly he wouldn't go to a dance until he was a lot surer his bad leg wouldn't fail him again in a pinch. If nobody showed up here to visit him, that wasn't his fault. Certainly it was no reason for anybody to call him a bunch quitter. With that self-excusing, he dismissed the matter temporarily.

Bad weather broke with little warning. It had grown colder, and Ragan one evening observed the low, ragged overcast that came rolling from the southwest. By night, lowering clouds had piled high and black on the horizon. In the night he awakened to hear rain pelt the earth roof. He smiled to himself, welcoming it. This was the kind of weather the Terrebine Cattle Company needed for its underhanded work. The change was a tonic that elated and energized him.

Storms and the showdown would come together. Both were near.

It was still raining at daylight, when he awakened again and crawled out of the bunk to dress. When he looked out the door, he saw the drenched flat, the mountains all about lost in deep mists. He turned back, built his morning fire, and had barely finished breakfast when a horse slogged into his yard.

His surprise doubled when he looked out the window to see Arch Terrebine swing down from a wet saddle. The man wore a slicker and rain hat, both streaming water. To have appeared here this early, he must have spent the night at Younts' place. He came toward the dugout at a brisk walk. Ragan moved over and opened the door.

Terrebine said, "Howdy, Chance. It's a hell of a day to go visiting."

"Any day's a poor one for you to come here, Arch," Ragan said, instantly aggressive.

Terrebine showed no surprise at the blunt truculence. He brushed past Ragan, entering the soddy. There he unlatched his slicker and shrugged himself out of it. He put it, wet as

72

it was, on Ragan's bunk, the hat following. Ragan promptly pushed the garments off onto the floor.

"You've outgrown your own shadow, Arch," he rapped. "Tall as you've made it."

"It riled you for me go up while you went down, didn't it?" Terrebine's handsome moist face was amused, his muscular body restless.

"Only the way it was done, Arch," Ragan corrected. "Why'd you come here?"

"It's time we made a dicker."

"This bad weather got something to do with it?"

"Everything."

Terrebine took a seat at the table, spread his thick arms forward and put his solid weight on his elbows. He was stirred by some inner excitement that Ragan found disturbing. Aware that he was suspected and despised, the man still had self-assurance.

"Start talking," Ragan said, "then get riding."

"You'll listen, and I'll leave when I please," Terrebine retorted. "Probably you've worried a little about Squint Lister."

Ragan felt a wave of cold climb up his back. It was a moment before he answered.

"What about him?"

"The story we're telling is that Squint seems to have pulled stakes."

"But he's dead?"

"Deader'n hell," Terrebine said with sudden force. "Murdered by Chance Ragan. And unless this high and mighty Ragan strings along, Squint's going to show up again. The sheriff will dig him up. Younts and Stub Nelson both say they heard you threaten to get Squint. They'll swear to it."

"And to why I threatened him?"

"Sure. Squint had reason to believe you been rustling up here. Fork's missed some stuff. Others might find they been losing cattle, too, if they checked up."

Ragan took a seat, partly because of the sudden weakness in his knees, but mainly because he knew Terrebine was here to stay until he got what he wanted. Ragan pulled out tobacco and began to spin a cigarette, holding his features immobile. The geniality that was in him often, of late, was gone completely. He felt a greasy fear in his middle. He could not prove that he had been justified in killing Lister. He alone knew that the man had meant to murder him in cold blood,

73

and he had no definite evidence as to who had made the other attempts on his life.

Arch Terrebine watched these things have their effect in Ragan, and he smiled quietly. He saw the cigarette, that got half built, remain unfinished in Ragan's stilled hands. The lines of his face lost some of their tightness as he savored his advantage.

"So I let rustled steers leak through here," Ragan said finally, "or I'm in trouble with the law. What else do you want of me?"

"That's all. Just go deaf, dumb and blind, and you'll be all right."

Ragan pondered that, stubborn, hunting his opening. Apparently, as Hanna and Dunsan had hoped, Terrebine believed his wintering the cattle up here to be a job made for him to help him out. Arch didn't seem to realize that Pace and Kitch suspected him and Younts of rustling. Ragan preferred to leave it that way, for their secret backing might be an ace in the hole for him.

"You know what I want to say to that, Arch," he said.

"But you won't say it. You don't dare."

"I reckon that's right."

Terrebine seemed satisfied. He rose, tall and solid, saying, "That lays the chunk for now. You're goaty, Chance, and I guess I don't blame you. You'll try to beat us even yet, and we'll figure on that. But you won't interfere with what goes on back here. You won't carry tales."

Ragan had not promised a thing. He still did not commit himself.

Terrebine took his time about donning his slicker and damp hat. He had barely reached his sodden horse when the animal showed interest in something south of the dugout. Watching, Terrebine let a puzzled frown build on his face. Ragan couldn't see from the doorway, but wondered if his bosses had chosen this kind of day to bring up feed for the stock.

Urgently, Terrebine said, "I'm hiding in the barn. You keep shut about me being there." He pulled back so that the dugout cut him off from whoever was coming in. He led the horse at a swinging walk toward the barn, where both vanished inside. In the rain, the fresh tracks were not evident.

Ragan stepped out into the yard and looked south. A horse was coming on swiftly through the storm. The small, hunched figure in the saddle suggested Nancy, although he didn't place

74

the horse. He stepped back out of the wetness because he wore no coat. A moment later the horse came in.

"Why, Joy!" Ragan breathed as he stared out at her.

She was wet and looked cold, but she smiled gayly.

"Didn't I pick a heck of a day to go riding?"

"You better light down and dry out. I'll put up your horse."

"Never mind," she said, swinging down. "I can only stay a few minutes." She dropped the reins and came toward the soddy door. Drenched as she was, she still looked lovely.

Ragan had forgotten the hiding Terrebine until a sudden excitement swirled through him. This was something for the man to see, as he doubtless was seeing through a crack in the barn wall. Letting Joy step past him into the dugout's warm interior, Ragan used the moment that her back was turned to swing a look about.

Rain by then had washed out the tracks of Terrebine's mount, blending them timelessly with all the others in the yard. Joy didn't realize there was anybody here but themselves. Ragan's pulses crashed in his ears as he followed her and pushed the door shut behind them.

10

JOY WAS silent while Ragan helped her out of her wet slicker. Then she pulled off her pork-pie hat to disclose dark, rain-curled hair. She wore a wool coat under the slicker, a turtleneck sweater above a divided skirt and a pair of tailored boots. She moved lithely to the stove, shivering but, like himself, warmed internally. He lifted the lid and poked in fresh wood, waiting for her to reveal the reason for this foul-weather morning visit. Its promise had him excited, stirring the male hungers that in recent weeks had grown with his strengthening body.

"I made up my mind to come last night," Joy said, realizing his curiosity. "And I wouldn't let a little thing like rain stop me. Didn't I tell you I was going to be your invincible counter-part?"

"Something developed?" Ragan asked, not liking that hint

of rancor, not wanting to let her lead them to another quarrel. They needed something far better than that; he wanted it with aching longing.

She shook her head. "No. It's the same old thing. I keep wanting to see you, and it's pretty plain I've got to make the moves. Are you proud you've done that to a Kildane?"

"Why should I be?" He was human enough to be touched by this odd humility. It seemed completely real.

Joy made a helpless motion with her long-fingered hands. "I thought about you all day yesterday. I decided I could stand to humble myself once more." She looked up at him, somber and wistful. "So here I am."

Ragan might have forgotten Arch Terrebine had he not sensed a shadow on the window for an instant. Her back was turned to it as she watched him, waiting. Ragan glanced at the window, but the glass showed nothing but rain.

Wonderingly, he said, "You're a woman apart, Joy. Your mind says one thing, your body another."

"And the body's winning, Chance. I've been frank about that. I'm tormented. I've got to have you. And I'm getting so I don't care how it comes about."

He swallowed hard. Each word she had spoken had been a tightening squeeze on a trigger within him. Then it shot through him, a driving urge that had in it less of sex than of bold and wicked vengeance. He stepped forward, sure of what she expected, and swept her into his arms. The rush of it made her tense, but only for a second. Then her hands found the back of his head and pulled his mouth onto hers, tugging hard and fierce.

"Damn you," she breathed, "but I can't help it. It's driven me crazy."

He swung toward the bunk with her, and she was limp as he placed her down. Then he glanced at the window again. It was still empty, but somebody had been there. He knew it. He looked down at Joy, who waited for him, her eyes closed, her breath running shallow and fast. She had meant her invitation. She was ready for what they both wanted, the proud Kildane brought at last to his bed.

And then the door burst inward.

Joy sat up with a choking outcry, aghast.

"Arch!" she said in a whimper that carried to the man who came in. Then she covered her face with her hands. But it was too late for her to save herself. She realized it.

76

She stayed there on Ragan's bunk, and the meaning of it could not have been any plainer.

Terrebine only snarled at the girl, then wheeled and lunged at Ragan.

"Damn you," Ragan taunted as he stepped back. "Don't you know when you're not wanted?"

Then he struck out at Terrebine to keep him from closing in. He landed a right fist that knocked the man back. Terrebine slammed against the door and grunted. He still wore his hat and slicker. Seizing the brim of the hat, Ragan jerked, pulling it down over Terrebine's forehead. He let go and planted his fist again in the man's belly.

"Now get the hell outta here," he panted. "And quit spying through my window!"

Terrebine cursed and clawed at his hat. He jerked it off and let it fall. Standing there panting, he managed to get out of the slicker. His eyes held pure murder.

"Arch, stop it!" Joy cried, her face uncovered now and streaked with shame and fear.

"Shut up, you bitch!"

Terrebine still didn't look at her, watching Ragan steadily, lethally, getting ready to attack again.

Joy moaned, then cried desperately, "I came here on my own initiative! It's none of your business, and you leave him alone!"

"It's my business, too," rapped Ragan, "and I don't figure to be left alone."

Terrebine's eyes were bright with outrage as he stood gagging for breath. Ragan seized the initiative and smashed into him again, sending another blow to Terrebine's belly. He had bewildered the man and kept hammering while Terrebine tried to cover up. He sent the man crashing once more into the wall. Terrebine made a wrenching shove, driving off the logs. He whirled and seized a chair and swung it high.

Joy screamed as he hurled the chair at Ragan, who bent and let it splinter on the wall in back of him. Terrebine kept cursing in a wild, frustrated flow of sound. He grabbed another chair and threw it in the same annihilating abandon. It missed Ragan and smashed into a shelf, bringing down the stacked cans there. The tins hit the floor with a crash and scattered everywhere.

Terrebine shook his head, his shoulders bunched, then the head began to wag from side to side. Ragan gave him another cool, goading grin. Terrebine leaped in, lashing out with both fists, drawing back, then steaming out and up. The blows caught Ragan on the mouth and skidded upward against his nose. The pain was sickening, and the force drove him against a wall. Terrebine lifted to his toes as he poured on his first steady, controlled attack.

Ragan knew a moment of sick distress. It seemed certain that he would go down. Covering, bobbing, he managed to evade the deadly punches Terrebine drove at him. In desperation he flung himself forward, his body bent and with a lowered head. His spring carried him through Terrebine's barrage. He hit the man's heaving chest with the toy of his head. He slammed Terrebine the width of the room, and it was the stove that stopped him.

Arch let out a cry, used his hands to regain balance and thus placed them on the hot stove top. He tangled his feet as he sprang away. The stovepipe came down as he fell, filling the room with soot and smoke and Terrebine's bitter profanity.

Blood streamed from Ragan's smashed nose, and he knew he was in another fight for his life. Terrebine meant to kill him as one male animal might destroy another, with the coveted female watching. It was fitting because she had not been had yet, Ragan thought. Almost, but not quite. Maybe, if Terrebine won, she would yield to him, instead.

Terrebine came up in a rush. Ragan shoved aside, but Terrebine deflected and came on, his drive scarcely broken. Ragan slugged wildly at the man's face. Terrebine lashed out with a foot, trying to catch Ragan in the crotch. Ragan stepped back from that in a narrow escape. He was gasping for breath himself, his lungs dry and burning. His strength was going fast. Terrebine struck out again, spinning Ragan against the logs of the wall.

Ragan's head hit a peeled log and fire swirled through his brain as if kindled by his red-hot lungs. He began to cough and remembered the smoke pouring from the dismantled stove.

Then Terrebine got his arms around Ragan, shoving him back onto the table, which in turn was impacted against the wall. The man began to bend Ragan backward, his knees and legs keeping Ragan's lower body upright. Ragan strained to break the vicious hold, to halt the thrust of a shoulder that seemed determined to break his back. He could hear Terrebine grunt from the strain as he tried again and again to do it.

78

Ragan's back kept bending until his belly was stretched painfully tight. He kicked, dragging back a foot and driving hard against Terrebine's ankle. The man's boot sole skidded on the floor. Ragan kicked again, and that time knocked Terrebine's prop from under him. The man dropped his weight onto Ragan's shoulders. But now Ragan stepped sidewise, moving out of that fearful, bear-hugging back arch. With a swing of his hips, he came free.

Terrebine came after him doggedly, again sending swift, slamming blows that Ragan could neither smother nor duck. Ragan would have quit, then, if there had been any quitting in him. He was finished. Wildness, a swirling jealousy over a woman, had brought him a fight he might have known he could not win. He fumbled. He hung on. And with blurred eyes he watched Terrebine grow confident.

Terrebine backed him into a corner and proceeded without mercy to belt him around. Ragan made one desperate try to get away from it. He shoved out from the wall and drove a slamming blow into Terrebine's face. It split the man's cheek, jolting back the sweaty, bloody head. But Ragan hadn't anything with which to follow through. The impetus of the punch carried him forward.

And then it happened; his bad leg let go again when he needed it badly.

He fell into Terrebine, who grabbed hold. For a moment the man seemed to rest on him, completely spent, in the same manner.

Then Terrebine raised his shoulder suddenly, and Ragan's gasping mouth clicked shut. The man put the full force of his body into it. Ragan's leg still wouldn't work. He went backward, dragging Terrebine down with him in a thunderous crash. Then Terrebine got astride him and started hammering at his head again. That was as far as Ragan could keep track of it . . .

When he regained his senses, the room was cold and quiet. The soddy door stood open. The rain cut past the outer light. Ragan was on his back and full of pain, of sickness and a racking shame. He was afraid to look further, for he had remembered Joy. On the bunk, her eyes lambent with her readiness to submit to him. He had no wish to see her looking at him now in what would be disgust.

Yet the door stood open. He could feel the draft and hear the steady drum of the rain. If she was still here, she would have had sense enough to close the door. He looked about, then, and suddenly was laughing. Sure enough, she had gone off with the visitor. He was all alone.

The wind that had chilled the place had cleared it of smoke. The fire had gone out. They had been gone quite a while— Joy and Terrebine. She had left with him, Ragan senseless on the floor, her near-mate beaten by a stronger one. She must have been in a hurry with Terrebine, too. They hadn't even bothered to close the door behind them.

Ragan looked at the bunk and kept laughing.

He got to a sit, but that was as far as he could manage. His face was a bloody mass. His clothes were nearly ripped from his body. He had taken one hell of a beating, which he had asked for himself. A year ago he could have killed Arch Terrebine in such a fight. Not now. Maybe never again. Suddenly Ragan stopped laughing.

He rose to his feet, bracing himself by the table that somehow still stood on its legs. Then, since he couldn't come fully straight because of the pain in his belly, he lurched out through the door in a bent-over crouch. The rain splashed on his hot skin, and he turned up his face and let it soak him.

He stumbled on to the spring and there began to scoop water in his hands and bath his feverish features. He kept this up for a long while, the strength of his body slow in returning.

He was still there when, without his realizing its coming, a wagon pulled up behind him. Somebody called, "Chance— my God! What's been going on here?"

Raban staggered to his feet and stood swaying. There was a team and wagon. There was a tarp on the wagon, and his numbed mind finally told him it was the winter feed he'd been expecting. The girl was Nancy, and Pace was with her this trip. Pace came down over the wagon wheel, his eyes blazing.

"Fellow dropped in," Ragan panted. "Wanted to argue, so we got at it."

"What man?"

"Pace—never mind."

Ragan rapped that out so sharply that Pace said no more.

Ragan walked to the dugout, letting the wagon pull along behind. He paused to dip water from the bucket on the bench, and he drank thirstily. He felt better, and he was damned if he would tell them how come he had got the hell beaten out of him.

He was ashamed of the reason now, as much as the beating,

80

ashamed to have Nancy's clean young eyes on him knowing how close he had been to intimacy with Joy Kildane. Above all, he didn't want her to know Joy had switched that feeling to the stronger man, one who had no game leg to betray him, who could fight for a woman and win.

Pace drove the team on toward the barn, Nancy still with him. They both had the sense to let him alone a while, and he appreciated it. They unloaded the wagon, and he used the time to try to straighten up the wrecked dugout. He skidded the cold stove into place and worked frantically to put up the tin pipe. He picked the litter off the floor and piled it any old way on what shelves remained on the walls. He looked at the two smashed chairs and laughed. There was no use trying to hide the work of a tornado. He let it go and began to kindle a new fire.

He had coffee started by the time Nancy came in alone. She said, "Do you know you'd ought to see a doctor? Your nose must be broken."

"Just spread out a little," Ragan said. "And I was tired of the way it was."

"This is twice I've found you messed up. Who is it you fight?"

"Just a man. For the crow-weight title of the Blues."

"It's Terrebine."

"Is it? There's lots of ambitious men around, Nancy."

"All right," she blazed. "Be proud and secretive. But will you ride down to Susanville and let a doctor patch you up?"

"No. Last ones who tried made a mess of it."

"Oh, you're bitter again! Whoever it was—goddamn him!"

He looked at her sharply, closely. She had felt that vituperation deeply, had brought it up from the depths of her soul.

He didn't object when she pitched in to finish cleaning the place up. She made the bunk over, and again he grew hot with shame. He was cool enough now to see why Joy might have turned so violently against him. Terrebine would have told her that Chance had known all along he was on the place. Such a thing would make any woman furious. It would even have a Nancy Hanna throwing things. His bitterness toward Joy diminished a little. She'd had a right to change sides.

When Pace came in, presently, he wore a look of forced joviality. "Get you one more load of feed up here before snow," he promised.

"Fine," Ragan said. "How did the cattle drive go?"

81

"Tedious, but no trouble."

The Hannas had had breakfast and expected to be home by noon, but they stayed for coffee. Since Pace was one of the men who had put him up here, Ragan wanted to tell him what had developed in connection with the cattle rustling. But now, for the first time, he remembered Terrebine's threat —string along or go up for murder. They could frame him, there was no doubt of it. So Ragan made no report to Hanna. Again he needed time to think.

He was glad when they had driven off with the wagon. They had barely pulled out when he toppled onto the bunk and let go, sinking at once into an exhausted sleep.

It was the dawn of another day when he opened his eyes again. His waking thought was guilty, that of a puncher—he hadn't taken a look at the cattle in his charge the day before. He tried to roll off the bunk with something like his old spirit but fell back with a groan. Yet it was only soreness that bothered him now. The fever had gone out of him, together with the roaring head. He turned gingerly onto his side, swung his legs out over the edge of the bunk and sat up slowly.

He could hardly move, and the torn knuckles of his hands made it painful to bend his fingers. He had slept in his ripped, bloody clothes, hadn't even pulled off his boots. He got up and staggered to the stove and managed to get a fire started.

There was coffee left in the pot, and he pulled the pot forward to heat. He got a can of beans but couldn't make his hands do the work of opening it. His lips were pulp, anyhow, so he probably couldn't eat if he tried. His nose was purple, swollen hideously, but he didn't share Nancy's fear that it was broken.

Just bent a little, he reflected. As long as both eyes aren't on the same side, I'm all right.

When the coffee was lukewarm he filled a cup. He fished out tobacco but couldn't manage the business of rolling a smoke. He drank the coffee black. With slow, sore movements he got into his sheepskin coat. The rain had tapered off, but a cold wind howled outdoors.

He went down to the corral and managed to get a saddle on a horse. He led it out and let it drink at the spring tank. He groaned as he swung up to the saddle, then rode out doggedly on the job he had been hired to do.

Ragged clouds still showed on the mountain ridges and the

sky was a dirty grey. The wind picked up a hum as it came
gushing across the flat. Its cold was painful to his battered
face. He rode with his head down when he could, but he
kept his eyes on his work. He'd had enough, for a while, of
foolishness.

He found nothing wrong with the cattle except for a few
inevitable strays—the bunch quitters. That made him remember he had promised Nancy not to become one of that breed.
Well, he had been set far back in his purpose of avoiding it.

He had to stay here, alone and determined. He had to
work harder than ever before. The day he knew he could kill
Arch Terrebine with his fists, he would take up his old life
again.

11

As HE came to the canyon that had led to the trouble with
Lister, Ragan grew tense. The mud in the passage was
tracked heavily. He knew at once that last night or the night
before a drive had been made, a rustlers' cut shoved up into
the hideout in the hills. The thieving was under way again.
Younts had grown sure of Ragan, unafraid of him since
Terrebine's threat and beating of a wasted, weakened man.

And what will you do about it? Ragan asked himself in bitter urgency as he sat his horse in the grey drizzle. Who'll
you tell? How'll you stop them without going to the pen,
yourself? He didn't know, except for one thing. He'd never
truckle to Younts and Terrebine. That knowledge was already a hardened fact in his mind.

Since the drive, the heavy rain had robbed the sign of
its freshness, making it harmless to Younts, and what evidence remained was swiftly disappearing. Ragan had no desire to go back to the hideout but he had to know what
brands had been taken there in the storm. He felt a mounting responsibility to their rightful owners even though they
might be men who had written him off as finished—no good
as a cowhand anymore.

Another look might solve a puzzle in his mind as to the
way Younts worked his neighbors' ranges, and even farther

afield, and the routes he used coming up here from the valley. Younts had to be caught in the act of stealing, so Ragan knew he had to take another ride to the rustlers' hole.

He realized it would be doubly dangerous, for his previous visit had probably induced Younts to post a guard up there. His decision made, Ragan searched his memory of the vicinity for a different way of getting to the hole so as to avoid, if possible, the chance of blundering into another trap. Younts had issued orders that he was to be taken care of at the first chance.

Presently he swung his horse to the right, going on along the flat where the hills crowded onto it in a long, meandering line. Later he slanted south, along a deep ravine with pine on the hills at either hand. The wind slacked off. The soaked earth was spongy under the horse's hoofs. The evergreens blended their fragrance with the newly washed air. The drizzle was just enough to be cooling to his sore face. His body was slack and aching but his mind was completely settled. As he rode, he pondered a deepening mystery. Ever since he had returned to hear how greatly Terrebine had expanded his cattle business, he had puzzled about the man's secret backer. He did not believe it was somebody out of Terrebine's past, as the man had claimed. His feeling was strong that it was a person or persons here on the John Day, somebody he, himself, might know. The thought roused a kind of unfathomable anger in him. A man had more respect for an open crook like Younts than for a hidden, two-faced traitor.

The backer could even be the main moving force in a scheme that was bleeding an unwitting cattle range to death. It did not seem possible that Younts could do the necessary financing, although he had come into the company. There was only one man in the John Day, and on intimate terms with Terrebine, who could do it—Judd Kildane. Whoever it was, he had to be rooted out and convicted with Terrebine and Younts. Even Judd, if he were guilty—Joy's own brother. He would hate that if it became necessary for he was growing sorry for the rough way he had used her.

An hour's riding brought him to a hogback he believed to be east of the rustlers' hideout. There he swung right, following a wet trace through tangled country marked only by the wild things that ran there. Shortly afterward his judgment was vindicated. He found himself on a bench east of the big hideout, whereas before he had inspected it from the west rimrock. The wind beat against his long, thin back. The teeth behind his sore lips were chattering.

The flat was still empty. For a moment he pondered that. He was sure he had not been wrong about rustled cattle being driven across Squabble Flat in the storm. Maybe the rustlers had decided this hole had grown too dangerous to use. Possibly the new cut had been small enough to be slipped in with the legitimately held cattle on Younts' ranch. Ragan leaned to the latter possibility. His enemies were too cunning to trust to their threat alone. They would make it as difficult for him to take action against them as they could manage. That was a sort of left-handed compliment to Ragan.

He turned back, feeling the weight of his disappointment. Once again upon the Squabble Creek flat, he made his usual long, encircling ride along its edges. The creek was shallow enough to be crossed at will, so that its banks were not apt to tell him a thing. The canyons would reveal nothing, either, because of the heavily weathered sign. But he poked doggedly, not starting back to the dugout until nearly noon.

He was hungry by then and had worked the malaise out of his punished body, except for the physical soreness that lingered. He attended to his horse, then cut across to the dugout and made his stiff, torn hands kindle a fire. The heat felt good and for a while he stood by the stove and soaked it up.

Afterward, slowly and clumsily, he cooked himself a meal and ate it. The food restored him surprisingly. After it, he mustered the patience to make a lumpy cigarette and satisfy the hunger for a smoke that had gnawed at him all morning. He remembered Joy, and then Nancy, and wondered why thinking of women could so sweeten a man's mind.

He was relaxing thus when a hunch-born idea came like a flash of light into his mind. Water, he thought. Mebbe there's ways they're using it I never thought of . . . He was instantly restless with energy, turning about the dugout floor in his limping stride.

One of the advantages of the whole great valley was its hill-born streams. Yet he was not thinking of the all-seasons creeks but of the washes that came into flood in heavy weather but otherwise went dry. With quick timing, a man could use a flash flood like an eraser to remove long stretches of trailing sign.

That would open up any number of ways to move stolen cattle through the foothills and into the higher reaches. Yet the insight only compounded the complexity of the situation. He poked at it a great while before he had narrowed the possibilities to the main probabilities.

Squabble Creek and its confluences were of great importance to Younts, as had been proved. He could come from far and wide onto the lower creek but needed the upper reach, with its narrow strictures, as the last link in his set-up. Pace and Kitch had suspected that. Terrebine had confirmed it by coming here with his threat. Chance Ragan was going to do something about it.

His cigarette went out in his preoccupation as he probed and poked at the question, and he forgot to touch a fresh match to it. Squabble joined Wildcat Creek—both shallow, sedimentary streams. Together, the two creeks gave access to every spread in this part of the valley, and fanned out toward more distant points in every direction. A man as intimately familiar with the country as Younts was—and as was Kildane—could see the possibilities in such topography.

Ragan caught up a fresh horse, saddled it and rode out at once, heading for Pace Hanna's Ladder. Strengthened by his hopes, he could again sit tall and easy in the leather.

He picked a new route, going down the gentle, meandering course of Squabble Creek itself. Although new to him, he found it to be as he had conjectured. At least at this stage of winter, a ridden horse could travel all the way down without difficulty, keeping to the water for long stretches and with only short obstructions to work around.

It was these occasional interruptions that crystalized his conviction. At places where downfall or short waterfalls blocked the way, he found cattle tracks, ageless as far as could be determined. He found cattle droppings of like deterioration, yet too much of it to be the calling cards of stray steers.

The chances were against one of the downcountry punchers finding a reason to make this same ride. So Younts had not worried over the few places where he could not avoid leaving sign. This, Ragan knew, was the weakness Pace and Kitch had hoped he could find. His resolve to use it to beat them was already hard as rock in his mind.

Possessed of the knowledge he had needed so badly, he pulled out of the creek to make better time, turning north toward the regular trail leading down into the valley. This would bring him out on Spade grass, and he decided to pick up Kitch Dunsan and take him over to Pace's place.

They had to set a trap on Squabble Creek at the next sign of a rainstorm.

Yet, as he came out of the hills, he began to grow dissatisfied with such a direct effort. The only ones it could incriminate would be those actually caught with stolen cattle. Younts would disclaim his riders or, if Younts were taken, Terrebine would desert him. The secret backer would be left in complete safety.

This led Ragan to consider another effort to which he had already given thought. There was the possibility of sending marked steers through the rustling system, serving as tracers that might prove the full extent of the operations. The answer, he decided, would probably lie in both resorts.

He found himself emerging into the valley at a point higher up than he had expected. Even as he broke out of the last draw to discover he was on Kildane's back graze, he discerned three horsemen coming along the foot of the hills. He would have whipped back into cover but realized at once that he had been seen.

The riders straightened in interest, staring his way, and Ragan recognized one of them as Judd, himself. The others were Teeter punchers, the necessary cogs for the big wheels in the rustling machinery. Although his presence here would arouse suspicions, Ragan decided on boldness as his best resort. He waited for them to close the gap.

All three gave his battered face a close, surprised inspection. His flat stare silenced their curiosity. "Man, you've had it," Judd breathed. "And you're sort of off your range, ain't you?"

"I tried a short-cut to Spade," Ragan said easily. "It turned out like most of 'em do. The next time I'll stick to the trail."

Judd eyed him with some deep speculation. It seemed to be dissatisfaction with that explanation. Or maybe Joy had told him of that primitive fight with Terrebine, if not its cause. Whatever, Judd did not like this.

Ragan tried to read what was going on in Judd's mind. If the man told Terrebine that Ragan had cruised Squabble Creek from the line camp down, Terrebine would know better than to blunder into a trap. But it would prove that Judd knew what the creek was being used for, which would be a gain in itself.

Judd wasn't going to betray anything now. He said, "See you again," and rode on, his men following him.

Starting his own horse, Ragan was thinking of the days when Judd had been his boss. The man had a strange, possessive interest in everything that pertained to Teeter. He knew his range count to the last head, his expenses to the last penny, and he kept a precise set of books on everything. If pennies could so obsess him, what would the thought of easy dollars do?

There was nobody at Spade but the cook, so Ragan rode on for Ladder alone. With his fall roundup finished, and his market cut sold, Pace was taking things easier. Ragan found him shoeing a horse. He swung down at the smithy door, stiffened again by the riding, nettled by this persistent handicap.

Pace looked up from his work, staring at him in surprise. He dropped the hammer he held in his sweaty brown hand. There were smudges on his blocky face.

"Man, howdy," he said. "This wins me a bet."

"How come?" The smile on Ragan's warm face was genial, as it was with few people now.

"Nancy said if we got you down here again, we'd have to rope and drag you. She put a five spot on it. Something wrong?"

"That's a question I can't answer yes or no. Younts made his first steal for this winter, either two nights ago or last night." Ragan eased his tired weight onto an old horseshoe keg and told Pace of the rustlers' hole he had found in the mountains, of his brush with Lister, and how he had been obliged to kill the man to save his own life. Finally he revealed Terrebine's visit and threat. But he said nothing of Joy and the real reason for the fight. Let Pace guess what he would.

"You been a busy little bee," Pace reflected. "And you should have gone straight to the sheriff, even if it gummed up our plans. They've got you over a barrel, now. It scares me."

"Got a little stomach trouble, myself," Ragan admitted. "At first, I couldn't make up my mind. Then I decided to let the sheriff come to me about it. Now I reckon it's so late it'd do me more harm than good."

"I'm afraid it is," Pace agreed. "You've got nothing to prove your story. Lister wasn't worth the powder to blow him up, but he can still get you into plenty of trouble."

"But there's so much more'n me involved, Pace," Ragan said urgently. "You and Kitch and all the other spreads that

88

are losing cattle. We got to keep after 'em." His set face showed his earnestness.

Pace went on with his work, saying nothing. He extracted a red-hot horseshoe from the coals in the forge and pressed it to the horse's hoof. The hoof sizzled and smoked and gave off acrid fumes. Pace was still silent as he began to whittle and rasp the hoof. He seemed to have drawn satisfaction from Ragan's declaration.

Presently he said, "So?"

"What's your opinion of Judd Kildane?" Ragan said bluntly.

"I got nothing on him, but I don't like him and never have. Why?" Pace looked up, his square face stirred and curious.

"Somebody backed Terrebine with a wad of dinero," Ragan answered. "Judd's got plenty. And the Kildanes are what you might call a trifle ambitious."

"You're cuttin' close to your own quick there, ain't you?" Pace asked quietly.

"Joy?" Ragan shook his head. "I don't know about her, anymore, Pace. I just don't."

"Then," Pace agreed, "Judd's the kind of stinker that'd back Terrebine, and I'm glad I can say it right out to you, finally."

"We got to get all of them, and why don't we take him into our confidence, or make him think so, and find out where he stands?"

"What you got in mind?" Pace asked.

"If he's in on the stealing, he seems pretty sure he ain't suspected. He'd be a handy way for us to get Younts to do something we could make use of."

"You got to cut the deck deeper than that," Pace retorted.

"I dunno how, just yet," Ragan said, "but if we could lay a trap and get Judd to trigger it, he'd prove he's in on the caper. You talk it over with Kitch, then come up and see me. Where's Nancy?"

Pace grinned. "This rain gave her a chance to catch up on her cooking. Go over and invite yourself to supper."

"Glad to," Ragan said promptly. He realized suddenly how much he wanted to see her.

He tramped across the sodden ranchyard, embarrassment mounting in him. Although she had seen him once since the

89

fight, he still felt disgraceful. He swung onto the porch, but she was at the door ahead of him.

"I saw you come in," she said tartly, "and bet myself a new hat you'd leave without coming over to see me."

"Then you're out a new hat and won one, too."

"I always hedge," she said, smiling. "Especially when betting on you."

"What's that I smell cooking?" he asked, a little annoyed.

"It could be cake, cookies or cinnamon rolls. Which'd you rather have?"

"All three," he decided.

"That's what I'm baking," she announced proudly. "Come and get it."

He followed her into the kitchen, his feeling of awkwardness vanished. It wasn't often he saw her in a housedress, like she wore now, a simple yellow cotton thing molded to her slim young body. Her apron was green. She had made coffee and there were fresh cinnamon rolls on the table that smelled tempting. He sat down and pitched in.

She took a chair across the table from him, pleased by his appetite. But she had a fish to fry, as well, and said, "Chance, you remind me of the man who left his shadow on the front porch and couldn't find it when he came outdoors again. He didn't realize the sun had moved around in back."

"I do?" he said, staring across at her.

"And you'll wind up the same way if you keep on hunting yours where you left it last winter."

"You're too deep for me, button," he snapped.

"Don't you call me a button!" she cried.

He looked up again, startled. She was really angry, and prettier than all tunket, to boot. The combination disturbed him.

"All right," he said. "I don't have sense enough to realize that things change. But, wise as you are, I don't agree with you. This thing goes back to where it left off last winter, no matter what's changed since."

"You're surely one-tracked."

"You bet," he rapped. "I've got to make any cow outfit on the John Day want me on its payroll. I've got a stallion that belongs to Angel Younts to ride. I've got Arch Terrebine to kill with my bare hands."

Her cheeks had whitened. He could hardly hear her when

90

she said, "And you've got a Joy Kildane to become worthy of?"

"Mebbeso."

He hadn't intended to say that, didn't mean it, and he stared up at her as she sprang to her feet.

"You are an obsessed idiot," she breathed.

"Now, Nancy—"

"Shut up before I start cussing. And get out of here."

"*You* cuss?" he laughed.

"You bet, you goddamn bunch quitter. Put down that roll and drag your freight."

She was so fetching in her temper that he stood watching her. She was dead right about him; deep in his mind he knew that very well. His wonder was as to why she cared, why this moved her so.

"You're pretty doggone wonderful," he said.

Her mouth dropped open.

"You can take the roll with you," she conceded. "But get going before I forget myself."

He was still munching the roll when he left.

12

RAGAN FELL to work on Squabble Creek with renewed energy, for the rain stopped and the clear weather prevented activity on the part of the cattle rustlers. The winter herd still gave him little trouble. But he found plenty to do and did it—hard, muscular work. He was still rankled by Nancy's currying.

His knuckles healed, his face with them. He rode up into the timber and cut more wood and banked it out. He cut enough poles to build the dugout into a fair-sized house. He drove the axe hour after hour because it worked him where he needed it most. He felt himself growing harder, stronger than before the fight with Terrebine. Yet deep inside he knew that he was a lonely man who would not admit his loneliness—a bunch quitter because of the pride in him.

One day he shaved for the first time in a week. When he was done with the chore he still looked like a hardcase because of his shaggy hair. He lacked scissors with which to trim it and decided to go down to the valley and visit the Susanville barber. Yet he knew this was only an excuse. He was finally honest about his feeling for his kind. He was lonely again. By going down to the mining camp, he would see only strangers, people who had not known the old Chance Ragan very well.

But he would go. Before he had left Ladder, on his last trip down there, Pace had given him his first month's wages. He'd cut loose his wolf a little and maybe stay overnight. He'd bring home his first hangover in a long while.

He rode into the mining camp in late afternoon. His eyes, as he entered, searched the muddy street for a barbershop. Spotting a striped pole, he reined in at the tie-rack in front. But first he headed for the adjoining mercantile where he bought a complete change of clothes. Entering the shop with his purchases, he soaked himself in its wooden backroom tub, then got his hair trimmed, exchanging a little idle talk with the barber. The wall mirror he watched was showing him the old Chance Ragan as he emerged from the thatch of hair.

His cheeks were tanned again, filled out, and his shoulders looked wide and meaty. The look of solid strength that appeared on his face restored the rugged good looks he had once been aware of without conceit. His nose had healed straight, the purple bruises had vanished. The sight was a tonic to him.

When he came out onto the plank walk, he felt better than he had in weeks. He put up his horse at the feed stable, wanting now to spend the night, and registered for a room in the Placer Hotel. He wanted a drink before he ate supper and also was curious about something he had noticed on the street—the front of a Terrebine butcher shop. Arch had no particular headquarters. He might even be here in Susanville tonight. And Ragan was stronger than at any time since his return to the John Day country. They might meet here, and Ragan felt ready.

But when he walked into the butcher shop he was mainly interested in seeing the kind of place Terrebine would run, now that he had achieved a monopoly. The establishment proved clean enough, was in no way unusual. There was a big showcase of meat cuts, a meat block on the sawdust-covered space behind it. Larger meat cuts hung on hooks and a door opened into a cooling room.

The butcher, heavy and florid, was busy with a miner, slicing a cut from a round of beef taken down from a hook. Ragan made note of the prices marked on the cuts in the showcase and whistled to himself. They were nearly double what they had been in his day in the business. Considering that a good part of this very meat had been rustled, he was impressed by the profits the new company must be earning.

And I almost died to make it possible for Arch, he thought bitterly. The desire to destroy this if he could stormed up in him.

The miner tramped out with his purchase, and the butcher looked at Ragan.

"Something?" he asked, in a voice showing his realization that he had no competition to beat. The reddish face wore a take-or-leave-it look that angered Ragan.

"That showcase," said Ragan, "is worth more than any mining claim in this district."

"Kind of high," the man agreed. "But we got to pay a hell of a price to the ranchers."

"That's what you tell the miners," Ragan rapped, "but I happen to be a rancher. I never heard of one getting a hell of a price for his beef from Arch Terrebine."

"You want some meat?"

"If I bought a chunk of that stuff, you know what I'd do with it." Ragan swung and walked out.

Night came, and the change brought the boom camp to its rowdiest. Ragan had supper in one of the restaurants, then strolled into the Bonanza Saloon, aware that he was less inclined to launch upon a town tear than he had anticipated. He felt better now that he presented a decent appearance but was a little bored with the camp already.

He had a drink at the bar, paying brief attention to the miners thronging the establishment, men whose lust for the precious metal had brought them to this isolated spot from all parts of the nation. They seemed alien to Ragan, whose passions ran as deep yet were fixed to more permanent ends. Rich today and busted tomorrow, or the contrary, was a philosophy that did not appeal to him.

The drink gave him little pleasure, and depression began to settle on him. Then suddenly his attention, now centered on the back-bar mirror, sharpened as he saw a young couple come through an inner doorway. The man was Kitch Dunsan,

93

while the girl with him was the prettiest Ragan had seen in the camp.

The two paused under the overhang of a stairway, in a cubby-hole formed by the inner walls. The girl raised on her toes and lifted her face to Kitch, who kissed her and looked around uneasily. The he hurried across the barroom alone and went out to the street.

Ragan felt an odd emotion stir in him. He had only a suspicion that there was anything special between Kitch and Nancy. Yet a swift anger came from seeing the man in this gold camp's flesh market. The girl Kitch had left now sauntered across the room, tall and dark and more quietly dressed than the others here. Nobody approached her, and she seemed indifferent to the whole scene. Ragan left his drink abruptly and walked toward her, wanting to know a little more about her and why Kitch would even look at her when he had a girl like Nancy.

She was at the foot of the stairway when he dropped a hand on her arm.

"Leaving us?" he said.

"Why not?" she asked, turning to look at him. Her voice was low pitched, pleasant, and the gray eyes that rebuked him were reserved and level. Quietly pulling her arm free, she started on. He knew he had tried to mess with something he knew nothing at all about. Suddenly he was uncertain about a lot of things, including Kitch and Nancy and, finally, himself.

He shrugged and went back to the bar.

A gray-headed miner standing in the place next to him looked at him with a dry smile.

He said, "Seems like you're new here, mister, so I better wise you up. That's Dixie Beauchamp."

"I'm supposed to be impressed by that?"

"At least warned. Her father owns this place. She sings here, but that's all. And, mister, I mean that's all."

"I'm warned," said Ragan. "And maybe also impressed."

He wheeled and left the place, the surge of wildness that had brought him to Susanville gone entirely.

He had headed for the feed corral to get his horse when he saw Terrebine and Kildane moving along the walk across from him. Excitement whipped through him. They were ahead and had their backs to him. He slowed his gait when the two, at the end of the block, cut a slant to his side of the street. They moved in to the horses strung at a rack

94

ahead of him. Instead of ducking under the tie-bar and emerging onto the walk, they halted by the horses as if getting ready to leave. They had not noticed him.

Ragan was close enough to hear Terrebine say, "Damn it, he's got to be away from there then. Joy's got to see that he is. She knows how. And I'm not so sure she won't like doing it."

At that moment Ragan came abreast of them. Light from a nearby window fell upon him as they turned their heads. Both gave a marked start of recognition, delayed, he understood now, by his grooming and new clothes and, above all, by the old physical attributes that had come back to him as a result of his dogged efforts. That insight was a brief pleasure to him.

"You've sure taken to straying, Chance," Judd said finally.

"That's what you said the last time." Ragan halted at the hitching rail. His gaze brushed Terrebine's face, but the man gave no sign of recognition. Why, I beat the son, Ragan thought wonderingly, with what I showed him about Joy. It was me who beat Terrebine. "Any reason why I shouldn't be here?" he added.

"None at all," Judd said. But he looked uneasy. He seemed to wonder if they had been overheard, which meant that they had been talking about him.

So Joy was to get him off Squabble Flat and in her own special way. He wondered why as he went on, his truculence put down for the moment by the development. His last doubt that Judd was Terrebine's secret partner had vanished. But he had to go easy until he saw what Joy was supposed to do.

Within ten minutes he was thundering out through the starlight toward the benighted hills.

He reached the Squabble Creek dugout too late to get much rest, but he stretched out on the bunk for the few hours that remained until daylight. When he awakened it was to hear the heavy drum of rain on the roof and to see it pelt past the window. It was the kind of weather in which the long loops swung on behalf of the Terrebine Cattle Company. He was instantly alert and active.

He ate a quick breakfast, saddled a horse, and had just swung up to leather when a rider came out of the misty pass at the lower end of the flat. Hoping it was Pace or Kitch, Ragan rode out to meet the man. But the visitor proved to be a puncher from Teeter, a gaunt, sour individual he knew only as Skinny.

The man tipped a gloomy nod and reached under his streaming rain coat for his shirt pocket.

"Got a note for you, Ragan," he grumbled. "And I'm to bring back a answer, if any. A hell of a day to play mail carrier."

Ragan accepted the sealed envelope that the puncher held forth. The writing was the same as had been on the note he received in Dalles City from Joy. His heart beat faster as he tore open the envelope and withdrew the message.

"I was forced to leave, the other day. I'm sorry for what happened, and I've got to talk to you. I'll be alone tonight. It's important to you, Chance. Come down and see me."

"The answer," Ragan said at once, "is yes. I'll do it."

The puncher nodded indifferently, having no idea of what was in the message and satisfied with that answer. With a parting motion of the hand, he swung his horse and was on his way back to Teeter.

Ragan did his outriding, which was uneventful. At the end of two hours he was back at the dugout, considering riding down to Ladder for another talk with Pace. But before he had made up his mind, Pace rode in, accompanied by Kitch Dunsan whose freckles were even more prominent on his wet features.

Drenched and blown by the strong wind, they tied their horses under the shed roof of the barn and came on to the dugout. As Pace shucked out of his rain clothes, he looked reserved and thoughtful. But Kitch was cheerful and seemed excited. Maybe he was remembering Dixie Beauchamp and the kiss she had given him.

"It's time," he said, "that we set up our trapline and see what kind of varmints we can catch. So we come up to make medicine."

"Set, men," Ragan said, feeling fine, "and we'll make it."

He poured the last of the coffee in the pot into the cracked old cups the dugout afforded, then set fresh batch of makings on the stove. It was good just to have company. He was about done with bunch quitting.

"You come up with anything new?" Pace asked. His heavy face was still damp.

"I think we got to try for one big knockout punch," Ragan replied. "From the way those polecats have talked to me, they don't seem to realize you and Kitch suspect 'em of

96

rustling. I had a idea we might send a cut of marked steers into their handling system."

"Working with the sheriff?"

"We'd have to," Ragan said ruefully. "You and Kitch could pick some stuff in good enough shape to attract Younts' eye, then mark and settle it on your back range real handy for him. Take a stylus and scratch the word 'rustled' on the horn of each critter, up where the hair would hide it. Have all Kitch's riders witness that, so they can back your testimony."

Pace nodded in approval. "Then, when the stuff shows up missing, we let the sheriff find it in the company's possession."

"It's that simple."

"But one hell of a gamble," Pace reflected. "And here's something you better know, if you still got an interest in the Kildane family, which I hear you have."

Ragan understood then why Pace was a little reserved with him. Nancy was still riled about Joy and his seemingly obsessive interest in her, which only increased his puzzlement about Nancy.

He did not deny that interest to Pace, saying flatly, "I know. Judd's in it up to his ears."

"And mebbe Joy ain't exactly ignorant of what's going on."

Ragan stared at him sharply. "You're taking a mighty long jump there," he rapped.

"Tell him, Kitch," Pace said quietly.

"Well," Kitch said, with reluctance, "I know a girl in Susanville."

"Pretty, too," Ragan said. "Dixie Beauchamp."

"How'd you know?" Kitch's freckles turned a full shade darker.

Ragan only grinned at him.

"She's purty," Kitch agreed, "her name is Dixie, and she's done a little spying for me. She sees and hears a lot of things in the Bonanza. Kildane comes there with Terrebine. They get to drinking and talking big. And Joy's been mentioned in ways that make it look like she ain't inactive in the business."

"I don't believe it," Ragan snapped.

"Sorry, Chance," Kitch said. "But I do."

"So," Pace said on a slow, long breath, "do you still want to set a trap for 'em?"

"For whoever's in it, by God!" Ragan answered.

"That's fine," Pace said in a low, angry way. "This country has been swindled and robbed. Judd throws a lot of weight, being the biggest operator on the fork. His example holds other ranchers in line for the company to steal 'em blind. Him and Joy put a lot of stock in position. But if we're guessing right, they've made a rotten use of theirs as leading ranchers."

Ragan could not deny that, even to himself. He'd heard Terrebine insist to Judd that Joy had to get him off the flat. Then had come that inviting note from her, which couldn't possibly have been a coincidence.

"Rotten as all hell," he agreed. "And something's set for tonight. I've been invited away from here pretty-please. I'm going to go, but you're going to stick around up here on the quiet. If I show up where I'm supposed to go, they'll figure there's nobody here. You do whatever seems necessary as soon as you find out what's up."

"Where you going to go?" Kitch asked.

"It won't be under any stairway," Ragan retorted.

Kitch shut up quick.

"They'll move cattle tonight," Pace reflected. "That's what it is."

"But something special," Ragan added. "When it comes to plain rustling, they figure they've got me hog-tied. This must be something they don't want even me to know. You two fixed to stay here tonight?"

Kitch nodded, and Pace said, "Nancy knew we aimed to make medicine. So if I don't get home right away, she'll figure it's got to do with that and won't worry. Much, that is. We'll stay."

"And we better clear out of sight," Kitch said. "This place is apt to be watched. We'll head for home, then cut back through the timber and hide there till dark. Then we'll slip back down here."

"Better eat first, then," Ragan said.

He cooked the noon meal. When they had eaten, Pace and Kitch rode out on the home trail. Ragan, knowing that the night might require much of him, stretched out on the bunk and slept a while. He awakened in the softening light of evening, ate cold food, and was ready to ride down to Teeter and his rendezvous with Joy as soon as it got dark enough.

Night came earlier at this stage of the fall. Ragan was soon astride the roan and dropping down into the lower

98

country. The rain kept up its steady drumming, promising that the dark hours would bring the action everybody wanted. Halfway down the long trail, he cut impatiently across country so as to approach Teeter by way of its back range.

The blackness grew thick about him for the sky was lost above the clouds that had brought the storm. Twice he had to rein in and figure out where he was. Then, at last, he saw the lights of Teeter headquarters dim and damp below him. He smiled grimly, wondering how Joy would cover the ugliness of their last meeting.

The big house showed light as he rode in, and so did the line of wet windows on the bunkhouse's near wall. Too much company, he thought with a wry grin at his secret excitement. He swung down at the yard hitchrack and tied his horse. The rain kept everyone indoors, and nobody greeted him or even seemed aware of his arrival. He went across to the ranchhouse at once and climbed onto the big porch. His swing was light and easy.

Joy answered his knock, not looking in the least embarrassed. He saw at once that she had dressed for him carefully, wearing a white blouse with a long black skirt. Her dark hair was upswept, her feet, peeking from under the skirt, were in light slippers. A subtle perfume touched his nostrils as he stepped into the hallway. It was, he remembered, the first time he had called on her thus in nearly a year. He had not dreamed that he would do so again, seeing her as he did now.

"Glad you came," she said, and smiled at him. "Awfully."

Ragan shrugged out of his rain coat and tossed it back onto the porch, his wet hat following. A curious sense of freedom was in him, of release. He owed her nothing, he had much to collect, and the night was full of promise. She was a woman who needed badly to be beaten at her own game. He needed just as badly to do it. She still stirred him, and only she could give him relief. He meant to have it.

When she had closed the door, he followed her into the long, antler-hung living room and its huge, glowing rock fireplace. There Ragan pulled up his shoulders. A man smiled at him from a deep chair by the fire.

"Howdy, Chance," said Judd, and he grinned.

"Evening," Ragan grunted, bewildered. If this was a rendezvous, it was mighty public. "And a good one to toast your shins, I reckon."

"So it is," Judd said ruefully, "but I've got to go out in that blasted weather. Joy said maybe you'd be coming over, so I waited to say hello. It's said, and I better get going." He rose from the seat, nodded and left the room, Ragan staring after him puzzledly.

Joy gave him a quick look of intimacy but was silent. His own tongue seemed tied, and he sat by the fire, warming his cold hands. Presently he heard horses move out of the yard, a number of them.

"Taking the boys with him?" Ragan asked.

"All of them," Joy answered, smiling bitterly. "We've got this place all to ourselves."

"What'll we do with it?" he countered, figuring a hiding was coming.

"Let's wait and see how it goes. We've got some things to settle." Her smile softening, she added, "You're uneasy, and I don't blame you. I was told to ask you down here tonight. It suited me to go along with the idea. I was furious over the trick you played on me up there. Then I realized you'd played it on Arch, not me. You made a fool of him, which is something he'll never forget. But you didn't have to do it. He knew before then you're the one I want."

"I figured you'd gone over to him for keeps."

"Pooh. I was through with him, already. I'd have stayed there with you if I hadn't been so mad."

"You seen him whip me."

"Because he had the advantage temporarily. By and large he hasn't beaten you and never will. He knows that as well as I do." Her eyes pleaded with him. "Chance, we've got to reach an understanding tonight. You don't deserve it after what you did to me, but I'm going all out for you. The time's come. I had to make that decision last night."

"Joy, you know what they're doing. The whole vicious thing."

She laughed. "And I've known a lot longer than they realized."

He got to his feet, but she rose quickly and came to him. Her face tilted up as her eyes searched his. She stood very close.

"Don't look so mad," she murmured. "All I've done is a little blackmailing of my brother. I still want you to drive Arch out of business. You're the one who should be in it with Judd, and I've forced my dear brother to accept that

100

himself. I've given him my decision. We'd both like to have yours tonight."

"I don't want in with him on anything," Ragan shot back.

"Then how about me?"

"Depends on what you've got to offer."

"Anything that you care to ask. Don't you know that already?"

He had to turn away from her and reach for his tobacco. He was fighting sheer, heedless impulse as he rolled a cigarette to keep his hands busy.

"Was the rustling Judd's idea in the first place?" he asked, not looking at her. "Was it him that had me drygulched?"

She shook her head. "He didn't know a thing about it until Arch came to him for the money to buy you out. I'm sure of that, or I could kill Judd myself. Younts is your man. Acting for Arch Terrebine."

"But I'm *your* man?"

"And always will be, my dear."

Again he had trouble keeping his hands off her lovely body. Her eyes, her words, her every expression told him it was still his for the taking. But there were more ways than one to use this willingness to give him what he asked. He had to keep his mind on them.

"What's up for tonight?" he said casually, getting on with that.

"Before I tell you that, I've got to know if we go on from here together."

"We don't."

He watched her features stiffen, her shoulders pull higher. Her confidence had mounted until his words seemed to hit her like blows of his fists. Her eyes narrowed.

"What are you going to do then, Chance?" she asked. Her voice was very quiet.

"End the rotten thing if I can. Certainly not take it over for myself. Not even with you thrown in."

"You can't kiss me and still say that."

"I don't aim to see about that. I want to know where Judd headed, and I've already got an idea."

He turned and was wholly unprepared for what happened in the same breath. He saw Joy's face change more deeply as she realized she had lost the game. Then her hand slid down into the neck of her blouse. When it came out it held a gun, a little peashooter that could blow out a man's brains as effectively as a .45.

101

"You underrated me," she breathed. "I was smart enough to hedge. You aren't trailing Judd. You aren't even leaving the house."

He turned back fully, his face wearing a smile that had little of geniality in it.

"I figured so. The question in your mind has never been between two men. It's been which one you'd rather have helping you pile up more wealth."

"You might as well sit down and be comfortable."

"If I'm not going back to Squabble Creek, why don't we go to bed?"

Shock jarred her features, then fury colored them. His eyes were mocking as he watched her, but his mind centered on that little gun. It was good for one shot, no more. His jeer still seemed to arrest her. He stepped in swiftly and slapped the gun aside, knocking it out of her hand.

She made a dive for it, and came down on her knees. He grabbed her shoulders, but she wrenched away from him, quick and surprisingly strong. She nearly got the gun before he caught the wrist of her reaching hand. Off balance, his bad leg buckled and he came down. He rolled his weight on her quickly, pressing her flat to the floor.

She kept twisting, her only sound a moan. She rolled her head as he dropped his mouth to hers, but he got her lips and pressed his kiss to them. He held her thus until she quit trying to get away from him.

"You can't take me and leave me," she whispered. "Go ahead and see for yourself."

He started to rise with the gun in his own hand, but her arms came about him and held him tight. Her mouth began a hungry hunt across his face, boldly seeking what was as old as life.

It was a long while before he rose, and when he spoke, he barely whispered.

"It's still so-long—for keeps."

He caught up the gun, hearing her torn gasp, "Why—you—you devil!"

But he was already headed for the door.

There was a dim light in the bunkhouse, but he knew that the place was deserted except for himself and Joy. He pulled on his drenched hat, got into his slicker, then went down to his waiting horse. The night's storm still roared over Teeter and the whole surrounding range.

It was the big night, he remembered, and he knew some-

102

thing else—he was really free of Joy Kildane. He had accepted her challenge and proved not only to her but to himself that her biggest guns hadn't been enough to prevent his leaving. That was worth much.

Moreover, she had confirmed the suspicion that it was Younts who shot his horse in the blizzard, at the urging of Arch Terrebine. That had brought on all the trouble, and a part of the trouble had already gone with her. Action now, and maybe he would have peace of mind again, would no longer be a bunch quitter but could take his full place in the John Day.

He tried to plan while his horse thundered on through the stormy night.

He knew Judd had waited at Teeter to be sure he showed up there where Joy could keep him out of the way. When he left headquarters, it must have been to join Younts in whatever was afoot this night. But none of them knew that Pace and Kitch were hiding on Squabble Creek in Ragan's place. He headed for the flat now, wanting to be there to help all he could.

Afraid to use the open trail, he again cut across country, imposing upon himself the task of finding his way through the black, rain-thickened night. A couple of times he pulled down his horse in uncertainty. Each time he was able to make out some landmark that gave him his bearings. Then at last he was in the clearing his own axe had made in the timber above the flat.

Sure of himself, finally, he rode on swiftly, dropping down to the flat just south of the line camp. The dugout was wholly dark, and there was no sign of activity on the flat. But it was still early in the night. It would be in the small hours of the morning when the rustled cattle got this far on their way to a dishonest market.

He reined in short of the dugout and called a low greeting to identify himself. When he was answered, he rode on in. Since Kildane had seen him arrive at Teeter, he doubted that a special watch was being kept on this place by the rustlers. But to be on the safe side, he rode up behind the barn, placed his horse inside, then kept carefully in the deeper darkness as he made his way on to the dugout.

He spoke again before he exposed himself at the door, calling, "Pace." Pace Hanna answered, and Ragan stepped inside.

13

THE FIRE had been allowed to go out. Without light the only sign of life in the place was the heavy smell of tobacco. Out of the obscurity, Kitch Dunsan's voice said, "You got back quick. What's the trouble—no stairway?"

"No—but plenty of trouble." With certain eliminations, Ragan told them how Joy had confirmed their suspicions.

Pace said, "If Younts needed Judd and all the Teeter riders, it's going to be a big haul. Seems to me we ought to do more than set here waiting for them to show up."

"Come around to that myself," Ragan agreed. "I wish there was time to get the sheriff here, which there isn't. But if you'll do some riding, Pace, and see every rancher you can between now and daylight, it might be all we need. Have 'em meet here the first thing in the morning. And Kitch had better hit for Canyon City and fetch out the sheriff."

"What'll you be doing?" Kitch wanted to know.

"That's what I want to make sure of," Pace added. "Don't forget Squint Lister, Chance. There'll be a ruckus if we take the ranchers to that hideout and they see wads of stuff they never got paid for. Hadn't you better wait and see who's left to tell about Lister before you bring out the sheriff?"

"I'm not the only one concerned," Ragan said promptly. "I'm ready to throw the whole works into the pot, make or break."

"It'll sure be make or break," Kitch agreed. "But you still ain't said what you'll be doing while Pace and me spank our saddles."

"I'll see what happens up here," Ragan said. "And try not to start my own ruckus. Now, you hombres get riding, and don't spare your cayuses. That bunch is pretty foxy at hiding hot steers."

The others got their mounts and left immediately. Ragan was feeling drained by then, physically and emotionally, but he was seeing straighter than he had in many months. He knew that the night's developments had multiplied the danger to himself. Joy would try to warn Judd that he wasn't having

104

any of their rotten prosperity. She was now his enemy, too, and would fight as hard as any of them to keep the profits rolling in. If the thing misfired, she would help them railroad him for the death of Squint Lister. That would be the residue of what she had called love.

At present there was nothing to do but wait and listen to the rain hit the roof, dull but distinct through the dirt. He wanted coffee to relieve his jadedness but dared not light a fire that might send sparks into the night. So he rolled cigarettes patiently in the darkness, as Pace and Kitch had done, and smoked them while he waited for something to happen.

He began to wonder if he would hear what he wanted in the increasing storm. Presently, when the middle hours of the night had come, he rose and donned his slicker and once more pulled on his sodden hat. He was confident that the cattle would come up along the bed of Squabble Creek, which now was running plenty of water for it.

He decided against taking a horse, for he would have to keep it quiet and wanted only to watch what went on. He left the dugout on foot. Keeping to the brush that ran out from the spring, he made his way up the creek.

There, at a wide point in the bed, he settled himself in the wet growth to wait once again. He grew drowsy and finally gave way to the half slumber that permitted instant awakening, which he had practiced countless times in the saddle.

Thus it seemed no time at all when, abruptly, every fibre of his nerve system drew tight. He had heard something. In spite of the storm racket, he had recognized the sound every puncher knew so well. Slow, heavy and unmistakable, it was that of massed cattle moving swiftly. He had gambled and made his point. Within minutes he was watching the first bawling, half-trotting animals hurry past him along the creek bed.

The extent of the gather amazed him, although he had expected it to be big. The point riders passed on beyond him, and it seemed a great while before the flankers followed suit. When the drive had passed him completely, he estimated the cut at two hundred head. Free beef for the Terrebine Cattle Company, worth twenty thousand in its price-gouging markets in the boom camps.

He kept place for long moments after the drove had passed him. The men with it were not needed in such numbers any longer, nor had they been needed since the cattle were thrown into the lower creek bed and started into the hills. That told Ragan that the collection had been made at scattered points. It had required a number of separate crews and spread the activity out enough that no serious depletion would be noted in any one vicinity. In the darkness he had not recognized a one of the men.

So Joy had not been able to carry a warning that would halt the operation. Now, warned or not, the rustlers would play hob putting the steers back on their proper range. They had committed themselves past turning back. They could only go ahead.

For fear that it would now be investigated, Ragan stayed away from the dugout. There was nothing more he could do until he had a force of ranchers to take in against the rustling outfit. He let himself doze again, wet and miserable and suddenly too spent to move.

14

HE AWAKENED to realize that dawn had washed away the seething night. Rain still pattered, as if the vapor that dropped it could never be exhausted. The wheeling flat showed its usual content of Spade and Ladder steers, already grazing on the new-washed grass. The rustlers had been careful not to mix the stuff as they came through. The movement had been as swift and skilful as it had been daring and vast. He stomped about, wet and miserable and altogether too tired for what he faced.

He knew that by now Joy must have given warning, which made him a badly wanted man. Every rider on last night's raid not presently needed to stay with the cattle would be hunting him down. There was a good chance he would brush with them before he could join up with the ranchers Pace was supposed to bring, men for whom he was gambling his freedom, his very life.

He was hungry and needed to conserve his strength. Anyhow, he was as safe at the dugout, under the circumstances, as elsewhere on the flat. But before he went there, he took another look along the creek. As the rustlers had planned, the rain and rising water had washed out all sign of a mass cattle movement. Nothing looked any different to him, and the irony of this emptiness burned the apathy out of him. He swung briskly down the creek.

Returned to the dugout, he fixed and ate a quick breakfast. He dared not risk the routine job of outriding his own cattle. But he watered the horse he was keeping up and tossed it some more wild hay. Then, finally, his close watching showed him a rider coming up from below. He stood waiting, tall and thin, but ready for what the day must bring.

He did not reholster his gun until he had identified Nancy. She rode hard, whipping into the outcamp and swinging off her horse as if all the urgency she possessed pushed her hard. The anger that had flared in her, the last time they were together, was gone completely.

"You're all right," she breathed. The brown eyes showed her deep relief as she and Ragan went inside.

Ragan laughed. "When did you find it out? The last time you figured I was all wrong."

"You know what I mean, Chance Ragan. Dad sent me. He's having trouble raising help. It's hard to tell when stock's missing, this time of year. They're all trying to check up before they'll believe Dad and go on the warpath about the rustling."

"All the lunkheads have to do," he snorted, "is come up and see their stuff in the hideout."

"It's a bolt from the blue to them, Chance," Nancy said. "You mustn't blame them for wondering who's gone crazy."

He realized the truth of that, in spite of his disappointment. The situation would not keep long enough for every plundered stockman to tally his herd. He cursed to himself, impatience boiling up in him. Canyon City was sixty miles away. Even if Kitch located the sheriff immediately, they could not get back before another day. The whole thing was settling on his own shoulders again. He accepted that.

Seeing the worry still on Nancy's face, he said, "You had your breakfast, button?"

The brown eyes flashed. "You call me that once more and I'll put a window in your head. So help me."

He grinned. "Nancy, I pretend you're too young for me so I can keep my hands off you. Now, wait a minute. I'm still under control."

"Shucks," she said.

He was aware that he had been drawn to her strongly ever

107

since his return to the John Day. Two things had kept him from realizing it, as she had known. He'd been obsessed—and she'd used the right word for it—with Joy and with what he had believed to be a great personal loss. Now he could see this yellowhead—very clearly and quite wonderfully. Joy would no longer torment him, and he didn't have to kill anybody to prove himself a man. He knew that with utter conviction, would never doubt it again.

"I didn't like it when you were down on me," he said.

"To be frank," said Nancy, "I wasn't really."

"What about Kitch?"

"I'll bite. What about him?"

"I figured—"

"I know what you figured. But he happens to be all gone over a girl in Susanville. I've been his counselor from the start. You could use one, yourself."

"Got one. She called me a goddamn idiot."

"At the time, she was right."

"She was," he said humbly. "When I went hunting for my shadow I stepped through the wrong door."

Her eyes were shining. He knew that she was running on lightly with her talk to cover deep and glorious things inside herself. He was too fresh from the arms of Joy to do anything more, now, than look at this clean, completely loyal girl. He wanted to tell her that he was free of Joy, that until this moment he had not realized why he had been able to walk out of her house forever without regret.

Now he only hoped that he would prove worthy of Nancy Hanna.

Then he straightened, listening closely to the outdoors. He wasn't sure, but it seemed to him that he had caught the sound of more horse travel through the low grind of the storm.

Bruskly he said, "I might have visitors. That would be bad for you, Nancy. Get on that cayuse and cut into the timber till I see who it is."

"I can meet anything you can."

"You get going."

She took the order meekly, moving outside. When she had swung onto her horse, she put it past the barn so she could head up into the pine. Ragan couldn't see the horses coming from the other direction, even then, but now was sure he heard them. A moment later, something broke out of the draw that had led him to the rustlers' hole. There were three riders, coming fast. Presently he had identified Younts and two Fork riders. They turned his way, and his breathing quickened.

He stepped back into the dugout, glad he had rushed Nancy off, and again he pulled his gun. They could give him trouble unless he got the drop on them and kept it until he had stood them off. But they moved boldly toward the dugout and did not seem surprised when he stepped out behind a leveled gun. He looked tall and ready and settled.

"Set quiet, boys," he warned. "Those are three saddles I'd admire to empty."

Younts looked drawn and tired, and his eyes were full of truculence. "Hear you got independent last night," he said. "Hear you kicked over the traces real big. Did you forget Squint Lister?" His soggy hat still set precisely on his hairless head.

"What about Squint?" The question chunked like a swinging axe.

"He's going to get dug up unless you come with me and the boys."

"What for? To get myself killed?" Ragan's smile was like winter light.

Younts scowled. "Don't look at me that way, man. You had your chance to play along, nice and safe. But you've taken it into your head to be ornery. So we've taken it into ours to trim your wick for you."

"It happens," drawled Ragan, "that I'm the one holding the gun. You might as well get riding."

"And you better come down off that high horse," Younts snapped. "We're still willing to make a deal. So come over to Fork and see Arch and Judd and make the best one you can get."

Ragan eyed him. "I've turned down better bait than that, Younts."

"Damn you, I ain't bluffing about Squint."

"You'll have to prove you're not." Ragan's lips grinned, but his eyes stayed cool and hard.

"All right, we will."

Younts drew back his head, then turned his horse and rode out, his punchers following. Ragan found some satisfaction in the fact that they had come. It proved that they still figured he was playing a lone hand and was the only one they had to beat.

Nancy soon came down from the timber. "I saw who it

109

was," she reported, "and you've never seen goose pimples like I had while I waited. What did they want?" All of her deep concern for him had crowded back into her eyes.

"Just tried to throw a scare into me," he said vaguely. "Now, you get home and make a cake. They still think I'm the only one they're bucking, and that's our ace in the hole. If Pace gets a war party together, tell him to hold it at Ladder instead of coming here. I'll get down sometime before night."

"Chance, you look out for yourself."

He laughed and watched her ride away. It was good to be a free man, to look forward instead of back. Whatever trouble yet confronted him, it was fine to know there were women like her in the world. She would stick with her man forever, asking no more than that he be truly a man. And he knew that he still was a man. That part of him had never been damaged, much less destroyed.

When Nancy had disappeared from the flat, he went at once to the corral and saddled his horse. Again he rode the full length of the flat, to its east end. Then he turned south along the shallow ravine that entered the hills. He was following the sign left by his own horse on his previous trip to the hideout, sign that was eroded now and rendered ageless by the storm.

The sharp fragrance of the pines reached his nostrils in strong drafts. He rode slowly, keeping a close watch all about. After an hour he was in the tangle of the hogbacks, heading westward. Finally he found himself on the high rim from which he had inspected this mountain-locked flat before.

There were plenty of steers on it now, the new gather, scattered across the flat and grazing. Ragan could see no riders but knew that Younts would have this herd under heavy guard. In case of trouble, and if warned in time, they would try to move it out of here. That made it necessary for him to know what kind of country lay beyond this section and deeper in the hills.

After a quick look from the rim, he pulled back from sight and then rode farther to the south. He was tight-nerved, worried, fully aware that he was the only outsider who could bring a war party in here. That doubled the price on his head, for he knew that Younts would not rely too much on the bluff about Lister. If they caught him where they had the upper hand, they would kill him instantly. This kept a

110

coldness in him but failed to slow his movements. His shoulders were back, held high.

Two hours of prospecting south of the hole told him there was nothing there to help Younts hide a herd of cattle the size of the one he had on his hands. Ragan turned back then. Younts was even more exposed now than he had dared to hope. Chance could plan now, and he already had a method well shaped in his mind.

If the stolen herd was jumped from the north end of the flat, it would be hemmed in by the hills. The vital thing was to have Terrebine, Kildane and Younts on hand to be surprised with it. He knew of one thing that would draw in all three—the pursuit of himself. He had to make arrangements with Hanna, then serve as a live decoy.

He swung wide of the flat, going back to Squabble Creek, wanting to run no more risks than necessary. He crossed the east end of the flat and pressed on into the pine beyond. He meant to circle the dugout, which might again be under watch, then make his way on down to Ladder.

Although this led him into unfamiliar country, he had no difficulty in making his way through the timber. In late afternoon he came out on what he knew to be Ladder range. Presently he was descending upon the ranch headquarters he had not visited since the day Nancy had raked him over the coals.

He knew from the lack of horses about the place that there had been no gathering of ranchers yet. He meant to change mounts, so he rode down and put the roan in the corral. Having seen him, Nancy came running across the yard.

"Dad isn't back yet, Chance," she called. "I wonder if something's happened to him!"

"What would?" he asked, noting the fear in her eyes.

"Nothing, probably," she admitted. "I'm just jumpy, I guess."

"Forget it and feed me. I'm plumb starved."

"All right." She turned back toward the house, relieved by his easy manner.

When he had watered and unsaddled the roan, he went up to the house. As he came into the warm kitchen, he saw that she had obeyed him and baked a cake to keep her mind occupied. It was on the table, fresh and fragrant, and a pot of coffee was hot on the stove. Ragan took a seat, feeling at home here now, feeling fine.

Pace rode in through the twilight. He had had even less sleep than Ragan and showed the effects on his wet, whiskery face and in his fatigue-dulled eyes.

"I been called everything." he reported as he warmed himself by the stove. "A fool, a slanderer and a plain lunatic. I never dreamed they were so muleheaded, and there wasn't a chance to get them together as early as this evening. But I set a deadline for tomorrow morning, Chance. Told 'em to collect here before then—sooner if they woke up to what was going on. Kitch ought to be back with the sheriff by then, too. But I don't know how many others will show up, if any at all."

Ragan was disappointed by that report yet not greatly surprised. A complacent man could be harder to budge than a bogged freight wagon. What the ranchers had been told had been a shock, a claim beyond grasping without some kind of proof. But right now, he knew, cow ponies were carrying punchers all over the range, checking up. He felt hopeful that many men would be on hand here before daylight, at least to talk the thing over. Whatever developed, he had to go ahead, even if it was still on his own.

In a sobered voice, he said, "Pace, you handle that end. Try to keep 'em bridled till we're organized and know what we're going to do. All you need is proof of what's been happening. This last batch of steers makes it. That, with compensation for what the cattle company has already rustled, is all they want."

"And what do you want, Chance?" Nancy said doubtfully.

"The same thing, plus."

"And it's the plus that scares the devil out of me."

He rose, saying, "I'll try to get Terrebine and Kildane up there, so badly mixed up in it they can't wiggle out. If you come in from the northwest, Pace, there's no way they can run them cattle to hide 'em. All you should do is tack 'em down till the sheriff shows up, if he hasn't already by then. I'll figure you'll be somewhere on the northwest end of that hole at daylight. At least with Kitch and the sheriff."

"I'll be there," Pace promised, "if it's all alone."

Ragan left, knowing that he was going to be on his own through much of the showdown. He was calm, set, but not otherwise greatly disturbed by the prospect. Change was coming to him swiftly now, a stability that he knew resulted from casting off old and useless burdens. One such had been a worthless woman, another the burden of bitterness over his long ordeal. The serenity born of this new freedom was healing him, he realized.

15

HE RODE south from Hanna's Ladder, not sure of his first objective. He faced the problem of getting Terrebine, Kildane and Younts together, then somehow drawing them to the rustlers' hole. He couldn't assume for long that they did not know the country was being aroused against them.

Some rancher or puncher, disbelieving, could go to Judd with a warning of what Pace was claiming and trying to get organized. If that happened, it was hard telling what the next hours would bring to the whole community.

The rain had dwindled, Ragan found, the overcast thinning so that the light was stronger than it had been the night before. But a wet saddle was never comfortable, and he rode in miserable fortitude, his mind busy. Kildane, he reasoned, would have pulled out his crew and returned to Teeter, his services no longer needed with the gather made and the drive accomplished. Maybe Judd was now home with his book-keeping, figuring up what the night had profited him.

But Terrebine would hang around until he knew how fortune was going to treat him, and he would be either at Fork or at Teeter. Considering how to get the three men where he wanted them, Ragan began to see a possibility. He was behind Kitch's place by then, and Teeter was on ahead. He decided to pay the Kildane headquarters another visit to see who might be there.

He lifted his horse to a faster gait. It was still early enough in the night for the lights of Teeter to show whether the place was occupied. A little later he saw light in both the ranch and bunk houses. He decided against prowling, which could be more dangerous than a bold and open visit. Loosening his slicker so he could get at his gun, he rode on in. His throat was dry and tight. No one here would welcome him, now, Joy least of all. But he felt they would not want to take an open hand in the dirty work that was Younts'

113

specialty and which was next on their schedule—the elimination of himself.

His arrival in the wet ranchyard excited no undue attention at the bunkhouse. Smiling sourly, he climbed the steps of the big house again. Once more he knocked on its door.

Yet he was startled when it was Joy herself who responded. For a moment she only stared out at him in her own surprise. Yet this time it was through eyes that were cold and bitterly hostile. The slim body was drawn up tight.

"Howdy," Ragan said casually. "Where's Judd?"

"What's that to you?" she asked.

He eyed her coolly. "It might be a good idea if I seen him, Joy. Him or Terrebine."

"You know what they'll do to you," she said fiercely, "if you come close enough again."

"And you seem scared of what I'll do to you if I get close enough," he said tauntingly. "Not this trip, lady. I'm in too big a rush."

Instead of flashing her wrath at him, she let her shoulders slump. She looked away, then back at him.

She said, "Chance, I made a mistake. All I needed and all I wanted was a man who can master me. I found that out when—when you did. Can't we start again? I'll help you fight them, even Judd. I'll go where you want, live any way you choose. Nothing matters but being with you. I'm sorry it took so long to find it out."

"Joy," said Ragan, "you can change sides much too fast."

Her shoulders came up abruptly and once more the dark eyes flashed. "All right," she breathed. "That makes it final, I guess. And you're right. I can change sides. I can love or loathe you. You despise my love, so you can have the other. I'll make you pay for what you did to me. Don't think I won't."

"Cash?" he intoned, reaching for his pocket. "How much?"

The feeling that streaked her eyes made him regret the sally. He had seen men look that way when they were about to kill. It was a shaking, offensive thing to see it in a woman.

"Men have been lynched for rape," she said bitterly, "and that's what you did to me."

"Joy," he rapped, "you wanted everything you got."

"Then why did I try to hold you off with a gun?"

He saw what a ghastly thing she could do to him if her pride let her expose that happening. He had struggled with and disarmed her, and then it had come about. Who would

114

believe that she had entered into it with all the hunger of a bitch in heat? Her eyes told him that this idea had come to her long before it had dawned on him.

"You scared to tell me where Judd is?" he asked.

"Why should I be? You'd be afraid to go there. They're all over at Fork. Go there, and I hope they kill you."

She stepped back and shut the door.

He realized that she could be lying. Judd could be there in the house, as could Terrebine, waiting to emerge quietly and try to capture him. Yet that did not seem probable. Few women answered the door at night if there was a man in the house. She had mentioned their intimacy, which she would not have done had there been somebody listening.

It was a long ride to Fork, but he mounted and started out again through the black night. He rode with redoubled caution since Joy might try to send riders to get ahead and waylay him or to warn them at Fork that he was coming there.

He reached the place where the fateful dry wash emptied into Wildcat Creek. It ran water now, a shallow but steady stream. Seeing it, he was reminded of his flight along its bottom, the time he had been forced to kill Lister. He didn't halt now but pressed on, in against the hills and drawing close to Fork headquarters. He was completely wary, and it was this that saved him, presently, when he noticed a sudden alert attention in his horse.

Reining in, he sat for a moment to listen. Horsemen were coming toward him at a fast clip, due ahead. They came from the direction of Fork. He studied for an instant, then swung his own mount about.

The closest cover was a brush clump standing at a considerable distance. He wanted to look at this party before he went on to Fork. He retraced his course for a ways, moving quietly. He came to a boulder nest where the wash joined the creek.

Moving in among the big rocks, he swung down. He stood at his horse's head with its muzzle pressed by his palm to keep it quiet. The clatter of running hoofs grew louder in the night. A moment later the party whipped past him, strung out and riding hard. He could have thrown any one of the horses or roped a rider out of the saddle. He was interested and puzzled, for Younts led the night riders. Behind him came Terrebine and finally Judd Kildane. The other two men were Fork punchers.

115

Dark as it was, Ragan was so close to them as they streaked past that he was positive of his identifications. Something had moved them fast and in force. He stood there, still silencing his mount, waiting for them to get on. Then he got a second surprise.

Instead of going on toward Teeter, as he had expected, the onrushing party turned up the wash toward the higher hills. Apparently they were moving up to the stolen herd, without effort on his part to tow them there. That only troubled him, for it hinted strongly that they had been tipped off, somehow, to the fact that they were to be jumped up there.

Presently he swung into the saddle and rode after them, still hearing the splash of running horses in the shallow water ahead of him. He kept within earshot, himself trailing where he had expected to be chased. He encountered no difficulty for what seemed a distance of two miles. He knew they would soon come to the fork where the ravine met the wash and led out to Squabble Flat.

It grew quieter ahead, forcing him to slow his own gait and ride with a more careful attention. Ahead, the hill on the left fell back a little. He knew it to be a chip of a flat where the important ravine came in from Squabble Creek. He stopped his horse, then, staring puzzledly.

A rope barred his way, a double length of hemp stretched across the wash. The sound of the travel ahead had resumed its full volume. He knew they had halted to string this rope, then had gone on. He pulled over to the side, then swung down on the bank. The rope had been put up hastily, tied to a cottonwood on his side and to a brush clump across. Then it had been run back to form a double strand, several catch ropes having been tied together.

For a moment he thought it was a spook put there to keep the stolen cattle from straying where they were not wanted. Yet the hard ride through the night suggested that much more was involved. There had always been the danger of the rustlers' getting wind of the suspicions mounting against them. This sudden alarm hinted strongly that it had happened, that they were trying desperately to cover their tracks. The Kildanes would insist on that. Teeter itself must not be thrown in jeopardy.

He couldn't decipher it all but knew this rope had been strung up to head cattle along a desired course. Its arrangement meant they intended to drive the stolen herd down onto

116

Squabble Flat. Then they could disclaim the evidence and try to make the rustling look like the work of the flat's known occupant. Something had certainly gone wrong to arouse them so deeply.

Puzzled as he was, Ragan knew what he would do about that. It was the work of minutes to loosen the rope across the wash. But the draw that joined the wash, which he next contemplated, offered no way to string the rope across it, as he intended. But the wash was open again, so he sat his horse in the bottom of the tangent draw and settled himself there to wait.

The night was now quiet, except for the fall of rain and an occasional moaning in the wind. Held motionless, he was soon uncomfortable, and fatigue settled in his back and shoulders. But he had a strong feeling that soon he would discern cattle coming down along the wash upon him. He meant to make them stay in the wash and give them an onward shove in that direction. Then they would spill out on range where they would be a re-doubled menace to the rustlers—Fork's and Teeter's.

The wait seemed without end. His horse swung its head and shifted its feet restlessly. Then, finally, both man and animal were listening. It was the sound of cattle, lifted off the bedding ground and being pushed where they did not want to go. Ragan recognized it but did not let his horse move out of its tracks.

At last he saw the point of the night drive ahead of him. There were no riders with it because the banks guided it, and the men expected their rope spook to turn the point up the draw and out to Squabble Flat. They would all be needed getting the bunch rounded in and funneled into the wash. So Ragan kept place doggedly.

The lead steers, as they came abreast, only gave the still figure of horse and rider a mild stare and kept to the wash. They were strung out in a loose file. He began to figure the time left to him, knowing that riders would soon be along. When they came close enough to realize something had gone wrong with their plan, they would be violently dangerous.

He kept a rough tally of the cattle moving past. When the bulk of them had plodded on down the wash, he drew his pistol. He fired three quick shots into the air, terrifying the steers. He threw his horse at the plodding drag, yelling like a Comanche.

The shallow water of the wash impeded the cattle, probably

would prevent a full stampede. But nothing was going to stop them now, and he had his own safety to consider. He swung his horse about and sent it pounding along the draw toward Squabble Creek.

He heard excited yelling, but it was at a considerable distance behind him. He had lost track of time but figured it would be hours before anybody could be on hand to help him. He knew also that nothing could now keep the stolen herd, or the greatest part of it, from spilling out on Fork's back graze and even on to Teeter's. It couldn't be rounded up in a night like this, or in half a dozen of them.

The pursuit that clung to Ragan confirmed his opinion that they realized that and would waste no time on the cattle. The place where their scheme had jumped the track would suggest unerringly who had been responsible. Now he began to consider his original purpose of playing hare to their hounds until help could reach him.

His horse had traveled a great distance already, and that worried him. As he rode, he replaced the empty shells in his gun. He recalled that once before he had been headed off and captured in this vicinity and did not mean to let that happen again. Weighing his plight with all the detachment he could muster, he decided not to use up his horse and himself in sheer flight. The darkness helped him, and there was only the racket of his plunging mount to keep them informed of his position.

Spilling out onto Squabble Flat, he swung west toward the line camp. Let them follow, thinking that he was preparing to make a stand in the dugout. That would be an advantage. He cut his horse in against the creek and its brush. Soon he came to a stop and swung the animal deeper into the cottonwood and its underskirting of thick brush. He waited again at the head of the horse, keeping it from whickering.

He could hear the pursuit, and it was coming after him without error. He grew interested in its volume, for he suspected that there were no more than two or three horses beating toward him. In all probability, the force of suggestion would carry them on to the dugout.

This switch of positions, he hoped, would give him a chance to make another move of his own. They cut past him, too far out to be recognized. There were only two riders, and they flogged their horses. They went on, thundering down upon the dugout on the west end of the flat.

Ragan waited through long moments to make sure no one

118

else was coming behind. The night again grew quiet as the hoofbeats pulled into the forward distance. Remounted, he went on, his mouth ruled into a flat long line.

His quarry was lost ahead of him. The fact that there were only two puzzled him. He feared that Terrebine and Kildane had pulled out, hoping to get away before they found themselves in grave trouble. Younts and his men could be left to try to save the situation. That failing, they would all bend their efforts to cover up. Those efforts could be as dangerous to him, Ragan knew, as this immediate situation. Temporarily safe, he was far from confident.

He felt certain the two men were going in ahead to investigate the line camp. He considered ways and means of having it out with them to cut the odds against him. He kept to the side of the flat, planning to come in upon the dugout from the bench behind. He held his horse down, so that its noise would not carry any distance.

Presently he swung across the creek and cut in to the south end of the long bench. He had no way of telling whether the two had ridden in on the dugout or had left their horses to approach it in stealth. Whichever, he wanted to climb the bench behind the place and, if he could, hand them a surprise. Gunfire might draw in others, but he felt a strong action here to be his best chance.

Climbing to the bench, he pressed in a distance from the rim and moved to his right. He was circling to get in above the dugout. It was here he had once captured Squint Lister, and again the ground swells kept him from seeing far ahead. At last he moved in over the low rise and at once stood transfixed.

A man shaped up ahead of him, and a voice called, "Stand right still, Ragan. I got you covered."

He didn't recognize the voice, and he didn't understand how one of the pair he had followed could have got up here without coming the same way he had. He had seen no horse in the area from which he had started up. Yet from his position the man had heard him and waited. Ragan still held his gun but realized he could not use it without being dropped in his tracks, whatever his own success.

Then the man lifted his voice, never taking his attention off Ragan.

He yelled in high glee, "Angel—I got the bastard."

16

RAGAN FOUGHT a wild impulse to have it out. From the way this man had called, Younts was on the level below.

"Drop your gun, Ragan," the man ordered. "This is the wettest damned wait I ever had. But it paid off. Been here since dark, hoping you'd show. Drop that gun, damn you. I want to go down and get warm."

Ragan let his gun fall. The man told him to move back, then came forward and picked up the weapon. Afterward he ordered Ragan to retrace his steps. Descended from the bench they rounded the springs and moved in toward the dugout.

Two men were in sight there. One of them, Ragan recognized as the distance lessened, was Angel Younts.

"Nice work, Curly," Younts commented. "Didn't I say that, given time, he'd get too smart for his own good? Ragan, I had a notion you'd fall out and let us pull ahead of you. You didn't know what I did—that Curly was up on that rim."

"And damned near drowned," Curly said. "Let's go inside and build a fire."

Beaten temporarily, Ragan let himself be shoved into the dugout. Younts thumbed a match and lighted a lamp. Ragan recognized the third man as Stub Nelson. They were all elated, confident. Curly moved to the stove at once and began to put kindling into it.

They all pulled off their rain clothes, so Ragan followed suit and was not stopped. They still did not know that Pace was due to arrive here eventually, maybe with Kitch and the sheriff and some valley ranchers. On the other hand, Ragan had no idea how long it would be until that would happen.

Younts dried his hands on the sides of his shirt and began to roll a cigarette. His hairless head, his blank cold eyes, made him look weirdly sinister.

He drawled, "Well, Ragan, you made us lose a pot but not the game. There was a fool rancher that wouldn't believe Hanna's yarn about us rustling. The cuss came to Judd about it. So we had to get rid of them steers but pronto. A temporary setback we'll soon make up for."

120

"And how'd you get rid of 'em?" Ragan taunted.

"It didn't do you any good to run 'em down onto us," Younts returned. "We're victims of a clumsy railroadin' job, that's all. It was you turned them steers down onto us, wasn't it? Well, it was you that rustled 'em, in the first place, Hanna and Dunsan assisting."

"All the ranchers aren't as foolish as the one that went to Judd," Ragan retorted.

"Mebbe not," Younts admitted. "We know about that meeting at Hanna's, too. Judd and Terrebine have gone there to bust it up. Judd can. He swings plenty of weight in this country. So you might as well relax, Ragan, and die in comfort."

"Die?"

"A dead man tells no tales." Younts laughed. "Or does he, boys? Maybe Squint could upset that old saying, huh? He's stinkin' dead, but he can still tell plenty on this smart Ragan." Younts licked his cigarette and lighted it, enjoying his first puff with an extra relish.

At the stove, Curly was helping himself to Ragan's provisions, setting out to make a pot of coffee. There was no mistaking that they considered their recovery worth admiring, figured on being back making money as soon as this scare had blown over.

"That sounds like some kind of bait you're setting out for me," Ragan commented. "What's next with Squint Lister?"

"You got any idea where he's buried?" Younts returned. Without waiting for the obvious answer, he chuckled and resumed. "Well, he's restin' in peace up there behind this dugout. We planted him one time when you was away from here. The way we see it, you must of been caught rustling by poor Squint, so you killed and buried him up there. It don't make any difference what Hanna and Dunsan have to say on your side. Nobody believes 'em, anyhow. That's been proved, already."

"I'll have my say, all right," Ragan snapped, but he was clammy with dread.

Younts shook his shining head. "Huh-uh, Ragan. The slickest tongue in the world never made talk once it was dead. You're a lowdown cattle thief, and you been rustling off of men who used to be your friends. You been around to see anybody but your sidekicks, except to hit 'em up for a job and go sorehead when they turned you down? Them ranchers are going to believe us, Ragan—that you finally went outlaw."

121

"You've tried to murder me before, Angel," Ragan reminded, "and it didn't work."

"This time we've got it fixed. We been suspicious about Squint vanishing and your skulking around in the backhills the way you done. So we come up here to look around and happened on a place where the rains made Squint's grave settle. So we dug and found him there. And he's still there, Ragan, for the sheriff to see. He'll take your carcass in with Squint's, because you caught us here and we had to shoot it out with you. See?"

"You cold-blooded devil," Ragan exploded.

"Don't blame you for not liking the idea," Younts said genially. "But that don't mean it ain't a good one."

Somehow Ragan managed a look of indifference, of contempt, but it was sheer, proud bluff. Younts' recovery of the night's fumble would strike raw fear into any man. It wasn't of immediate importance whether the man could make his account of things stick. He thought he could and would act on that belief. Ragan knew he stood a slim chance of leaving the dugout alive. He had to bluff, and it had to be more than looking disdainful and defiant.

He managed an easy voice when he said, "You're dead wrong, Angel. Since I don't run off at the mouth like you, I'll let you wait to find out why."

"He still thinks he can beat us, boys," Younts said and laughed again.

They seemed to be in no hurry, and Ragan knew now that he had no hope of help coming to him from the valley ranchers. Terrebine and Kildane might not be able to break up the meeting at Hanna's, but they could throw it into confusion and uncertainty and forestall any conclusive action.

Still casual, Ragan said, "Since that's my coffee your man's cooking, supposing I have a cup?"

"Give the man some Arbuckle, Curly" Younts told the puncher at the stove. "And the rest of us can use a little. I don't really hate you, Ragan. Not the way Terrebine does. You know how it all started. He had to get rid of you, and there was Joy to boot. He knew you had the inside track, that you could still have it if you'd take it."

"He can have her and the cattle company and welcome."

"He can have her," Younts agreed, "but he's got pardners when it comes to the company. My price for fixing you was a piece in the business. When Terrebine went to Judd to get the money to buy you out, Judd wanted in. You know him.

A regular damned bloodhound when it comes to smelling a dollar. Terrebine's a weakling. You ain't. Sort of a shame you couldn't swap places, at that. I think I'd like it better, myself."

That was odd, Ragan reflected. Terrebine's only assets seemed to have been his strategic position and willingness to go crooked. Each of his confederates would have preferred Ragan, if he had been in the same position and possessed of the same dishonesty. Arch Terrebine knew that. Regardless of passing triumphs, he had been beaten again and again in the one way that counted—the testing of one man against another.

Ragan drank his coffee and smoked a cigarette. Still trying to bolster the confidence he showed, he said, "There's one thing I'd advise, Angel. Before you crawl out on a limb by killing me, make sure Squint's body is where you figure. It happens the rain did what you said you'll claim. It settled the new dirt on him. I'm up on that rim a lot, going to the timber where I been cutting wood and poles." Ragan stopped, grinning.

"What do you mean?" Younts demanded.

"Your yarn wouldn't sound half as good if you couldn't produce what's left of Squint."

Younts came forward in his chair, his eyes narrowing. "You moved him? Ragan, that's so plain a sandy you ought to be ashamed of yourself."

"You care to murder a man without making sure?" Ragan asked. "If it wasn't me you mean to beef I'd let you go ahead for the laugh."

Younts didn't believe him, nor quite disbelieve him, either. His plans were dangerous, and he couldn't ignore the possibilty that Ragan was not bluffing. Looking at one of the punchers, he rapped, "Stub, you go out and see if Squint's still there."

Stub gave a start. He flung a glance at the dark window. He swallowed and said, "We got no shovel. I ain't going to dig him up with my hands."

"Then root with your nose," Younts jeered. "But make damned sure Squint's where we planted him. Ragan, if you moved the carcass, you had to have a shovel. Where is it?"

"Barn, but Stub's scared to dig for a dead man on a dark night. See him shake in his boots? I don't blame him. Squint was a mean one alive. His spook'd be twice as ornery. Stub never helped Squint the day he got killed, you know. Mebbe Squint remembers and is sore about it."

"You shut your goddamn trap!" Stub yelled.

He hunted up Ragan's lantern and lighted it, turned grumpy and nervous by the macabre work assigned to him. He got into his raincoat and fiddled with his hat at the door.

That amused even Younts, who said, "In case you find him running around in his bones, Stub, just yell for help. Mebbe we could get up there in time to save you. On second thought, you better go with him, Curly. Let a horse bust wind, and Stub'd be on his way to California. I could spare him, except he's the one who heard Ragan threaten to kill Squint."

Curly didn't like the prospect, either. He scowled at Younts, started to object, then broke under the man's flat stare. Ragan's chest was so tight that he had trouble drawing his breath. All he wanted was to get their minds off him for a few minutes. He seemed to be succeeding. Right then Stub and Curly were busy dreading the job, and Younts was enjoying their discomfort.

As a parting shot, Ragan said, "Some men don't take to having their grave opened, boys. Specially on a wet, cold night."

"Thought you said he ain't there," Stub growled.

"Wasn't, the last time I looked, but he might be sentimental about his old one."

Ragan was seated on his bunk, then, and he watched the two men go out into the stormy night. Younts had taken one of the chairs and was between Ragan and the door. He wore his gun on the left side for a quick crossdraw. In spite of the horseplay, he had placed a hand prudently on his lap, within easy reach of the gun.

He grinned as he observed Ragan's interest in that weapon. He was at ease, seeming pretty sure that Ragan had bluffed about moving the body. A man positioned as he was would be hard to overcome, and he knew it.

Ragan hoped to upset that complacency in the most disconcerting way possible. While Younts had been amused at his men's superstitions, he was not likely to be free of them, himself. Nine times out of ten the vicious ones were cowards in the face of the supernatural. That was the result of the guilt in them, maybe.

Without warning, Ragan said, "By God, Younts, you shouldn't have made light of Squint's ghost!" He flung a hard, open-mouthed stare toward the window at Yount's back. "There it is coming up on you!"

The man couldn't help himself. Given more time, he might

have figured it out. As it was, he reacted by instinct, twisting to swing a look at the window. In the same second, Ragan sailed off the bunk.

His hand had for long moments been closed on the hard, straw-stuffed pillow there. He swung it as he moved, hurling it at Yount's face. The man ducked and lost the chance to use his firearm.

Ragan was on him, driving Younts and the chair over backward with a heavy crash. Ragan's first effort was to clamp a hand over the man's mouth and shut off an outcry. His other hand caught the gun in a powerful grip.

"A long while ago," he said in a panting breath, "I swore I'd kill the man who dropped my horse in the blizzard. You admitted it was you, Angel."

He shut off the man's mouth and nose with his hand. Younts threshed in mighty wrenches, but Ragan held him, feeling no mercy. Younts used his free hand trying to break Ragan's grip. He gouged at Ragan's face and clawed at his eyes. Finally he managed to free his face enough to draw in a gagging breath. He never got enough air to let out a yell. Ragan stifled him again, and Younts' effort weakened. At last the man went limp.

Knowing he could not finish the job he had for one raging moment set out to do, Ragan rose with Younts' gun in his hand. The man was so highly dangerous that he bent and whipped the barrel across the inert man's head. He lifted him, put him on the bunk and pulled a blanket over him.

He realized presently that he had plenty of time. Stub and Curly had not rushed about finding his shovel and putting it to work. Resting from his tangle with Younts, Ragan waited another ten minutes. Presently he saw the lantern swinging across the rainswept yard, coming toward the dugout. He crossed to a place beside the door.

He fell behind the door as it swung open. He heard Stub's startled exclamation at the sight of the empty room. When the door closed, he had his gun covering them.

"Strange goings-on, boys," Ragan drawled. "Angel up and vanished into thin air."

"Where is he?" Curly gasped.

"Did you find Squint?"

"Hell, yes, and knowed we would. Where's Angel?"

"That's him making the lump on the bed. We're going to get horses, boys. You'll strap Angel to his saddle. Then we're all going down to that meeting at Pace Hanna's."

"What for?"

"To sort of counteract what Terrebine and Kildane might have done."

17

HORSES STOOD in numbers in Hanna's ranchyard. A lantern hung on the end of the hitchrail threw the place into mixed light and shadow. The house was bright with several lamps, and as Ragan rode in with his prisoners he could see the shapes of men outlined against the windows.

Younts had revived by then but, in spite of his steady cursing, Ragan left him strapped to the saddle. The two punchers, cowed by Ragan's gun, had offered no resistance coming down from Squabble Creek. Their arrival attracted no special attention, for newcomers had been showing up all night. Ragan herded his charges to the edge of the porch and shouted.

The door swung open. A man looked out curiously at the figures disclosed by the light from the doorway.

"Hey, Pace!" Ragan yelled. "Come out here! I brought you a present!"

That drew not only Pace Hanna but several others. The porch had filled by the time Ragan swung out of the saddle. He tightened his shoulders as he glanced upward at Arch Terrebine, just coming through the doorway uneasily. Judd Kildane was right behind him. There was some pleasure for Ragan in the shock that jolted across their faces when they interpreted the scene below them.

"That's right, boys," he said. "Angel muffed it again. If you didn't use such cheap help, I'd be proud of myself. Pace, hasn't the sheriff got here?"

Pace shook his head. "Kitch ain't showed up with him." He came on down the steps and looked at Ragan. In a discouraged voice, he added, "Chance, they've about got you hung. Terrebine and Kildane have lied from start to finish. They've made it stick with these lunkheads. They've got the whole country in the palm of their hand. After what's happened, I'd say welcome to it, except they've got you framed. Where did you latch onto these polecats?"

126

"At the dugout. You better let Angel down before he busts a blood vessel. Don't worry, I aim to keep my gun ready."

Hanna released Younts, who all but collapsed as he came down from the saddle. His two men helped him to his feet. He stood there glaring at Ragan. His confidence was restored by what he had heard and the presence of Terrebine and Kildane.

"Ask him how come," Younts blazed at the crowd in general.

He slid his furious glance over their faces and wet his lips with his tongue. The group was comprised of nearly every stockman in that end of the valley. Ragan knew with a dismal feeling that they were on Kildane's side, on Terrebine's—the two men they thought had brought them prosperity.

"If you ain't going to ask him," Younts resumed, "then I'll tell you. Me and the boys have been worried about Squint Lister. And wondering. Some of you knew him. He up and disappeared, a while back. There was reason to suppose he'd lit his shuck. Stub there knew Ragan had threatened him, and Squint was scared. But he was a tight-fisted cuss, and he had pay on the books. It seemed to me he'd of collected and said he was pulling his freight. He had no reason not to."

"I've heard this before, boys," Ragan said to the crowd in general. "It gets better as Angel warms up to it."

The angry look in the eyes on the porch and steps made him glad he had kept his gun on the trio he had brought in. Now he held it so he could cover anybody else who forced his hand. They were dying hard, these people, convinced that they had been rustled poor but wholly confused as to who had done it. He didn't like the feel of things a bit.

Arch Terrebine took up the play, saying, "Get to the point, Angel. What were you doing on Squabble Flat?"

"It's quite a story," Younts said, "and I'll have to tell it all. You recollect, Arch, that Ragan hit me up for a job. I made him one because I was sort of sorry for the cuss at that time. I sent him off with a cut of steers to take to Dixie. He was back the next day with a yarn about losing 'em to rustlers. I didn't swallow it. Me and the boys checked the sign. Them steers he lost had been driven into a hole in the hills. We found 'em, and there were other steers there. All kinds of brands." He looked about. "You boys were all represented. The dirty son had nicked all of you."

"Why didn't you tell us?" a man yelled at him.

127

"Figured it better to keep quiet and watch Ragan. But I told you at the time, Arch. Remember?"

"That's right," Terrebine said promptly. "And I told you, Judd."

Judd caught the play and nodded. "Sure. I remember."

"So I let Ragan go," Younts resumed. "Told him I didn't need him any longer, so's not to make him suspicious. Next thing I knew he showed up on Squabble Creek. Working for Dunsan and Hanna. That looked mighty odd. There'd been sign that rustling had gone on even before Ragan come back to his country. We got to wondering if Dunsan and Hanna weren't helping him with it."

"Why, goddam you," Pace growled and took a step toward the man."

"A guilty man always acts touchy," Younts taunted. "And the men Ragan went to work for are the only ones in the valley who'd rather drive to a far-off market than sell to the cattle company. Why? Could it be that made a way to get rid of rustled steers? Ask Hanna and Dunsan."

Ragan could hear a pulse crash in his ears. A deep cold cut through his body. He was not the only one they were trying to make the 'scapegoat for the aborted rustling activities. They intended to drag Pace and Kitch into it, too. That would at least discredit them and weaken their testimony. They were playing for a second chance to betray the confidence of the men who listened.

"Get on with it, Younts," a man called.

"You're hearing bald-faced lies," Ragan warned. "But go ahead, then you'll learn the other side of it."

"Well," said Younts, "me and the boys got to wondering if, instead of running, Squint had bumped into trouble we didn't know about. Stub here remembered hearing Ragan tell him to keep his mouth shut about something if he didn't want to get ventilated. Mebbe Squint seen or done something else Ragan didn't like."

"Let's forget the mebbes," the same man rapped. "What happened?"

"Well, we decided to take a look around that line camp today. Went up there aiming to ask this Ragan a few straight questions. He wasn't there. But we looked around and had a piece of luck. You know that slope that comes down from the rim behind the dugout? Well, Curley stumbled onto a funny little sink in the ground. We dug in, and it was a grave the rains had settled. Squint was in it. He's still there for the

128

sheriff to take charge of. That's it, boys. Make up your own minds about it." Younts grinned ruefully. "But the crafty son sneaked up on us and threw down and here we are."

"You might as well put away that gun, Ragan," Terrebine said. "Unless you figure to light your shuck right now."

"I've got no such hankering," Ragan retorted. "But maybe you'll have one."

"I'll tell you what he's leading to, Arch," Younts cut in. "When he seen us on Squabble Flat, he knew the jig was up. He run them stolen critters onto me and you, Judd. Fool enough to think that would make it look like our work. And that's the size of it, men."

"I say it's enough," a man yelled. "The hell with waiting till the sheriff gets here. I dunno about Pace Hanna. I trusted him till he got to talking and acting so crazy. But this Ragan. There's not only the rustling, but his laying hands on Joy Kildane. I say we ought to string him up right now."

Hearing Joy's name, Ragan felt a sick quivering in his stomach.

"Not while I'm holding this gun, Sam," he said softly. "Hate to say it, but I'll use it on any man who makes a false move. You've got your minds made up, so there's no use wasting my breath. I could go right now, if I wanted to. I've got the drop. But I'll stay and take my chances if you'll wait and let the sheriff handle it." He had stepped back and swung his six-shooter so he could cover them all.

Pace stood stunned. He could offer no help for he was unarmed. This was his own home, and he'd had no inkling of what was going to develop from the meeting he had called.

Pace looked miserably at Ragan and said, "What sunk you, Chance, is that Joy got them breathing fire and brimstone before you reached here. Claims you caught her alone at Teeter and misused her."

Ragan nodded. He hadn't believed she would actually bring their private affairs into it. But so great was her hatred she had done it. She had said the one sure thing to get the men in the country up in arms. She figured he would let himself be swung up before he would divulge what had really happened between them at Teeter, how badly she had wanted him at the time.

"Do you believe that, Pace?" he asked.

"Hell, no," Pace snorted. "But they say I'm a rustler, the same as you, and my word's no good."

"Joy here now?"

129

"In the house."

"Tell her to come out here."

But, apparently listening, Joy appeared in the doorway voluntarily. She looked coolly down at Ragan. Yet he could read the taunt in her eyes, her daring of him to go ahead and violate his natural chivalry. She knew he couldn't do it and was taking advantage of that knowledge.

She said, "He'll deny it, of course. Perhaps claim I led him on. But I had to tell you the kind of a man he is, to protect my brother."

Even he had been inclined to lay bare the fierceness of her passion, Ragan knew it would only add fuel to the outrage burning about him now. "The woman did tempt me and I did eat," was not accepted in the cow country.

Standing close to Ragan, Pace whispered, "She's got you fixed, Chance. Light out while you got the drop and surrender to the sheriff on the quiet. I'll tell him you're going to when he gets here. But don't get caught or you'll be strung up."

Ragan nodded miserably. He wished he had a fresher horse. He handed the gun to Pace, whispering, "Cover me while I get aboard."

Pace swung the weapon back on the watchers. His eyes had a frozen glint, his voice was low.

"Everybody stand quiet. Ragan will surrender to the sheriff, and so'll me and Kitch. But there ain't going to be any lynching. You're going to stand like wooden Injuns till I tell you otherwise."

Back in the saddle, weaker than he had felt since his return to the John Day, Ragan looked for a long moment at Joy. It was she who broke gaze, and he wondered what effect that would have on those who observed the fact. Then he rode out.

The best thing, he knew, was to head straight for Canyon City, hoping to meet Kitch and the sheriff on the trail. He realized that, at best, he was in extreme peril. They could make that false story of Younts' stick in court, enough of them hanging together on it. He now had no doubt that Joy would testify against him there, as she had here, simply to blacken his character sensationally and help make the charges seem valid. That was the measure of her revengefulness.

He was still within earshot of headquarters when he heard the muted crack of a gun behind him. Fear slashed through him, not for himself but for Pace. He dared not return unarmed, so spurred forward, wondering if Pace had been forced to shoot somebody or had been overpowered.

When he pulled down again, a few minutes later, he heard the sound of a horse running after him. Even before he started on, the volume swelled. Others had joined the chase. He had been obliged to leave his .45 with Pace, feeling that the only danger to him in all the country was concentrated at Ladder. Now he regretted it and had only what remained of the night to throw them off his trail.

His horse was too worn for him to outrun his pursuers and meet up with the sheriff and Kitch. It was now doubtful if even the sheriff could give him protection. His knowledge of the backcountry byways might help him escape, except for the questionable endurance of his horse.

Moreover, he was now deeply worried about Pace, and this was what changed his plan. Knowing the temper of the cow country as he did, he was sure every man who had been at Ladder, excepting Pace, would be in the saddle and coming after him, out of misguided chivalry as much as personal affront. Maybe the smartest thing he could do would be to double back to Ladder, cautiously, and at least get a weapon, a fresh horse and some food to carry with him. That also would give him a chance to see what the shooting had been about.

He swung from the trail and plunged at once into the thick brush of the creek. He forced his horse into a rough crossing of the stream at a point where the animal did not want to tackle it. Emerging on the far side, he cut back toward Ladder, taking his time to let them all clear out.

He reasoned that Younts, Kildane and Terrebine would lead the chase, whipping it on. Although they had the cards stacked against him they would still prefer to see him dead and unable to act on his own behalf. That was the kind of respect they had gained for Chance Ragan, whom they had treated with contempt on his return to the country.

It would be possible for them to kill him now with impunity. He had made himself a fugitive from what at least a dozen men would swear was justice. It would be with them, as it must with him from now on—shoot on sight.

He heard the thundering hoofs fade out behind him, and slowly he drew in upon Ladder headquarters. He dismounted in the timber at some distance and made the last approach on foot. Coming up at a corner of the barn, he paused to make certain that the yard was empty. It was, yet he continued to move with care, calling softly as he neared the house.

"Pace—Nancy—it's Chance."

Nancy appeared in the doorway, then ran toward him. She didn't hesitate a minute about throwing herself into his arms. "What happened?" he breathed.

"Younts and his men jumped Dad. He only got off one shot and it went wild. Then they overpowered him."

"He hurt?"

"No. He's in the house. They only mauled him a little."

"I got to have a gun and a fresh horse and some grub."

"Don't go in the house unless you want to see Joy," Nancy breathed. "She's still here. Her gallants were so hot after you, they went right off and left her. Personally, I'd like to bury her up there with Squint Lister."

"I want to see her, Nancy. She lied in her teeth."

"I know that. But nobody else does."

"She does. You let me see her alone."

"All right," Nancy said with a sigh. "But I'm not going to like it much."

Joy was seated in a living room chair, looking drained and worn, when Ragan walked in. She must have heard and recognized his voice, for she did not seem surprised to see him. He stopped before her and looked down for a long, long moment. She would not look up into his face.

He said, "I never dreamed it was in you, Joy."

Then she did look up, angry, defiant, proud. "I didn't lie. You took advantage of me, a dirty, unfair advantage. You knew I loved you and used it for your selfish pleasure."

"I took nothing you weren't all too ready to give, Joy. And if loving me is turning me as rotten as Judd and Arch, then I guess you did."

"What would you call it?"

"Pure greed. The same as you feel for money, for a position high above your neighbors."

"Is that all you wanted to see me for—to cheapen me some more?"

"Joy," Ragan rapped, "you were born cheap, or you wouldn't have brought up that private thing at all. Judd doesn't believe you. Arch don't, after what he seen you ready to do on Squabble Creek. But the others did, lock, stock and barrel. Innocent and abused men you're crowding into something they'll regret all their lives."

"They'll hang you, and I want to see them do it."

"And that's love?"

"What's left, after you betrayed it."

132

18

STARING DOWN at this woman he had once wanted, of whom he had dreamed so much on lonely rides and in quiet nights and especially through the long months of waiting to see the doctors would leave of him, Ragan had a sudden sense of never having seen her before. Her hatred had brought many things to the surface of her face to stand in bald ugliness as she contemplated him in return. Passion, greed, vengefulness, and a streak of cruelty a foot wide. Beauty and a viciousness deeper than original sin.

In a strange, unearthly way his mind went back again to the days when he had ridden for Teeter. Once more he was seeing Judd poring over the ranch books, accounting for his possessions, his gains and losses in the minutest detail, letting nothing escape the cold, possessive precision of his mind.

The hunch came to him then, strong and compelling. He had assumed that Terrebine would have been the company bookkeeper, as he had been in the days of Terrebine and Ragan. But Judd Kildane would not trust to the reports of Terrebine or Younts in business matters, nor the dozen butchers in the retail outlets—nobody but himself.

The books're on Teeter, Ragan thought with a surge of excitement. I got to get hold of them—now, while everybody's out chasing me.

Joy rose from her chair then, as if she meant to leave.

Shaking his head, Ragan said, "No you don't, Joy. You're staying here a while longer."

Her chin came up. "Oh? And who's going to hold me here?"

His hand on the softness of her breast pushed her back into the chair.

"Pace, come here!" Ragan called.

Pace came in from the back of the house, looking puzzled. Nodding to Joy, Ragan added, "The lady's getting restless, but I figure she better stay here till we're sure she can't get in another dirty lick."

"If you say so she stays here."

133

"And if hanging her up by the heels will help, I'll fetch the rope," Nancy added from behind her father.

Nodding, Ragan turned and headed for the doorway. He saw that the rain had stopped.

He rode straight for Teeter, figuring his enemies would be beating the country for him between Ladder and the hills. The stars were soon out in gaudy brilliance, the air was warm and scented by the washed wildness of the countryside. His fresh horse moved at a steady lope.

The total darkness of Teeter headquarters told Ragan that the whole crew had been taken to Hanna's to back Kildane's hand at the stockmen's meeting, and was now out on the chase. But to guard against the chance that the old cook or wrangler was on hand and sleeping, Ragan left his horse short of the building site and covered the last distance stealthily, on foot.

He was glad of the time he had put in on this ranch, which had given him an intimate acquaintance of every foot of it. Judd's office was in the big house, which was why it had been necessary to keep Joy from returning here from Ladder. No ranch house was ever locked, and Ragan stepped inside at once when he had mounted the steps and crossed the porch without any sign of disturbance at the bunkhouse.

Within the space of three short breaths he was in the office. He closed that door carefully behind him and knew at once from the total darkness that he would have to risk lighting a lamp. He drew the blind on the room's one window, trusting that thereafter anyone seeing illumination within would figure that Judd or Joy had come home. He thumbed a match aflame, then touched it to the wick of the oil lamp on the rolltop desk.

He looked about with a wary exhilaration stirring through him. There was an iron safe in the office from the old days when Teeter had operated on a cash basis. But it had not been used in years, its lock was rusty and its door stood slightly ajar. He turned his attention to the cluttered desk.

The ranch books were in plain sight, but he knew that Judd would keep a separate, more secretive ledger to account for the affairs of the cattle company. He began to go through the desk drawers one by one. At intervals he paused to listen through a long moment, but the night still was quiet. He searched the last drawer of the desk without finding what he wanted.

Frustration had begun to nettle him when his gaze settled on the old safe. Crossing to it, he swung the door full open.

The interior showed a dusty litter of old account books and letters, nothing more.

There was only one place left to look, the old pot-bellied stove that heated the space in winter. With a wry grin he walked to it and opened the creaky old door. There he found what he wanted.

Under a layer of wastepaper was a small pocket-size account book, fairly new. He drew it out with bated breath, his hands trembling. Crossing into the stronger light by the lamp, he thumbed the book open. He knew at once that he had Judd's secret figures on the new cattle company. There was a page for Arch Terrebine, for Younts, for each of the butcher shops in the mining camps. The whole thing was there, set down in a precise hand.

Judd Kildane had remained in character, even in this dangerously dishonest undertaking. A quick inspection was enough to show Ragan that he had kept a record of every steer delivered to the butchers, together with the money turned over to the owners by the shops' local operators.

This'll do it, Ragan thought in triumph. The company can't show bill of sales for all the stuff they've turned over to the butchers to sell. We've got 'em.

He blew out the lamp in haste and, clutching the book, began at once to move toward the door. He had not quite reached it when he halted. A horse was coming in toward headquarters, moving fast. He wondered if Joy had somehow gotten away from Ladder.

He cut out through the back way of the house, waiting outside the rear door until the horse had thudded into the ranch-yard and come to a stop at the front porch. If the light that had showed through the office blind had been seen from the distance, suspicion would be aroused already.

Then a fist was thumping on the front door. A voice yelled, "Joy—you here?"

There was no mistaking that voice. It belonged to Angel Younts.

Ragan stood motionless, sucking in slow and shallow breaths.

Younts did not yell or rap again, and the silence was eloquent to Ragan. The man pausing to consider, which meant that he must have noticed a light in the house. Ragan slid on then through the darkness, rounding the corner of the woodshed, then cutting off into the obscurity beyond. He had to

135

move half around the house to reach his horse. He did it slowly, carefully.

Already he was considering his next move. This revealing account book belonged in the hands of the sheriff. But beating the country in search of the officer was too dangerous an undertaking. He would have to return to Ladder and, with Pace's help, stand off any enemy that might show up before the sheriff got there.

When he reached his horse he could turn and see the front of the ranchhouse. His blood pumped harder when he saw the light, again, in the blinded window. The cat was out of the bag, already because Younts had been shrewd enough to go there immediately. He knew the one thing a prowler would be after, the most dangerous thing—thanks to Judd's machine-like head—to the new cattle combine. Maybe worry about it had brought him here.

Ragan decided that he had to wait and see where Younts headed from here. That would give him an idea as to his own best procedure.

He was still standing there, staring out through the night, when he saw a figure appear on the big house porch and run down the steps. Younts rose immediately to saddle, hardly seeming to touch the stirrup. He swung his horse about and was gone at a clatter. Swinging up to leather, then, Ragan followed him.

A little later he was puzzled, for Younts was striking a beeline toward his own ranch. The fact renewed Ragan's decision to dog him and see what else might be revealed. The man had received a distinct shock on learning that the account book had been taken. His haste, now, indicated that he figured there was something he had to attend to immediately.

Ragan was so certain Younts was heading home that he fell back so as not to betray himself to the man. Swinging over a little to the right, he began to pick his own course, far enough off that he could again hurry his horse.

Even so, he came down on Fork to see that the place showed light. That surprised him, for most of Younts' men had been with him throughout the course of that night. Once more Ragan left his horse at a distance and went in on foot, using brush and buildings to cover him. A heaving horse stood at the house steps, Ragan slipped the account book under his belt to free his hands, then drew his pistol.

Presently he had reached a place where he could look

through one of the dirty windows into the bare, drab house. He saw two men come through an inner doorway into the main room. He felt a tingling bewilderment in the back of his neck.

The man moving ahead of Younts was Kitch Dunsan.

In that moment it was clear why the sheriff had not reached Ladder. Kitch had never got to Canyon City. They had been looking for that and had taken him prisoner. Younts had held him here on Fork, but the loss of the account book had frightened him into thinking he had better move Kitch away from his own headquarters.

Then a voice behind Ragan rapped, "What you trying to see in there, cowboy?"

There was only one thing to do, then, and instinct did it for Ragan. The voice belonged to the old cook on Fork, the man who had helped saddle the stallion that nearly killed him. Knowing the man would be armed, Ragan whirled and shot. The cook's gun seemed to fire in the same split second. Ragan felt the slug rip through the side of his shirt. He could only see the man vaguely. He was about to trigger again when the figure before him lurched sideways, then went down.

Younts was yelling, then the light in the house went out. Ragan pinched his lips into a hard, flat line. Luck had been with him for a little while, but it was all gone now. He had to get Kitch out of Younts' clutches, and Younts would put up a desperate fight.

Ragan was already moving, running for the back corner of the house. That proved a poor choice for, as he rounded it, a gun ahead of him blasted the night. He jumped back, aware of how close he had come to being shot head on. The gun barked again but harmlessly.

Feeling it better to reassure Kitch than to keep Younts puzzled, Ragan yelled.

"Kitch—it's Chance!"

Kitch's answering shout was echoed by another pistol shot.

"If you got that cussed old cook, there's only Younts left!" Kitch called from somewhere in the interior. "Get him, man—get him!"

Ragan knew that was easier said than done. For a second he stood puzzling. Then, swinging, he began to move up toward the front of the house. He had a strong feeling Younts had fired that last, useless shot to lend the impression he was waiting there. Then the man would try to slip around and get in behind his foe. Ragan's eyes were narrowed, his tread careful and light.

He came around the front of the building to see his man coming on toward him. Younts spotted him in the same breath. No word was passed between them for none was needed. Ragan saw Younts' quick stiffening. He was thinking of that blizzard night when he fired. He heard the gun blast echoed by the other weapon. Something red hot touched his side and he was twisted half around.

Frantically he fought to control his balance, swinging back. It was to see Angel Younts take a running step forward then lurch and go down. The man tried to shove up on stiffening arms. The arms collapsed, and then he was still.

Even so, Ragan went in warily. When finally he stared down at Younts' back he knew it was all over between him and this one man. Gingerly finding the man's wrist, Ragan made sure. There was no pulse. Had Younts not panicked there at Teeter, he would still be alive.

"All right, Kitch," Ragan called quietly. "He's got."

Kitch moved stiffly as he came out of the house. Ragan did not have to be told that he had been tied up for a long while, held motionless. Kitch looked down at Younts, shook his head, and had nothing to offer.

"So they nailed you," Ragan commented. His side was stinging, but he realized he had only been burned across the ribs.

"Before I'd gone two miles," Kitch said ruefully. "A couple of Younts' tough twisters. What's next?"

Ragan tapped the account book still safe under his belt. "I got what we need against 'em here in Judd's own handwriting. That's what put Angel into such a sweat. He figured he better not get caught holding you a prisoner, too. Wonder what he meant to do with you."

"Beef me, that's all," Kitch said bitterly. "And I'm damned glad somebody around here's got a brain or two."

"I had a hunch, that's all. Come on."

"Where to?"

"We're going to make sure Kildane and Terrebine are still around to explain something. Namely, how they come to have so much more beef than they ever bought."

"Where'll they be?"

"Right now they're chasing me. All I got to do is show myself someplace, and they'll be there quick. Best spot I can think of is Ladder, with Pace there to side us."

19

THE WHEELING stars showed Ragan that it was two hours past midnight. It seemed certain that, once the futility of beating the hills had been realized, the hunt would be called off until dawn. That would be no more than another two hours. His pursuers would then return to Ladder to pick up his sign for a more thorough and relentless effort.

As he rode through the starshine with Kitch, Ragan was busy with this thinking. Pace and Nancy would hold Joy at Ladder until they knew it was safe to let her leave. There was more on Ragan's mind now than inflicting a physical defeat on his enemies. The Terrebine Cattle Company was indebted to a score of ranchers for a substantial sum of money. The killing of Terrabine and Kildane, though justified, would not square that account.

They reached Hanna's ranch with very little of the night remaining. Pace and Nancy in the kitchen with an extremely truculent Joy. There was a pot of coffee on the stove, cups on the table. Pace had filled a saucer with cigarette stubs. Stepping in with Kitch, Ragan noted the shock in the Hannas' faces when they saw who was with him.

"Where in hell's the sheriff?" Pace asked finally.

Kitch made a weak grin. "I been playing pattycake with myself at Fork. I reckon the sheriff's snug in his soogans about now."

"Nancy," said Ragan, "how about herdin' your girl friend into the other part of the house?"

"Anything to help," Nancy said, rising from her chair. "Come on, Joy. I'll show you my hope chest."

The hostility that streaked Joy's eyes was not good to see. She tossed her dark head.

"Go ahead and be smart, Nancy Hanna!" she blazed. "It's only temporary!"

"Honey," said Nancy, "you just get a wiggle on that ruined carcass."

When the girls had gone into the other end of the house, Ragan lowered his voice and told Pace what had developed since he left Ladder so hastily. He put Kildane's account book on the table. He showed the others how it proved that the cattle company had furnished its outlets with far more beef than it had bought from the ranchers.

"That nails 'em," Pace said with satisfaction. "It's the weakness we've wanted to find all along. Coming out of Judd's own nature, too. It just ain't in him not to keep books on everything that goes on, to make sure he don't lose a penny he don't need to."

"It's more than a matter of sending 'em over the road, though," Ragan reflected. "Those buggers have made a potful of dinero out of their beef monopoly. I say they can make amends to the outfits they rustled from. That's something a criminal court wouldn't do for them."

"How do we do it ourselves?"

"That so-called posse's going to be back here in the first light to try and pick up my trail," Ragan said. "Me and Kitch'll lay low. When they show up, you're going out and fetch Judd and Arch in. You can tell 'em you're holding Joy, and they better come and powwow before she spills all their beans for 'em. That'll bring 'em."

"Fine," Pace agreed promptly. "What then?"

"If we get an offer to square up, we'll take it."

"In return for dropping the case?" Kitch gasped.

Ragan shook his head. "In return for my not pressing and proving, which this book helps to show, that they tried three times to murder me."

"You don't hate 'em so much now?" Pace said softly.

"Hate 'em, yes," Ragan said, "but not the way I did, Pace. I found out that getting revenge don't undo what a man's suffered. But justice is another matter, and we'll have it. Now, you two go in and keep that wildcat spread-eagled. I want to make some private medicine with Nancy." He looked at Kitch. "That all right with you?"

"All right?" Kitch intoned. "Man, it's way past time you did."

The two men vanished through the inner doorway. Nancy was back in the kitchen immediately. All at once she looked quiet, demure, and in a matter of fact way she poured herself a cup of coffee.

"Well?" she said, looking over the cup rim at him.

"To begin with, I love you."

"Good beginning, but not enough."

"And I'm asking you to marry me."

140

"What am I doing with this coffee?" she cried, and dropped it as she ran toward him.

Ragan knew in that first real embrace that he had reached the right goal, however different it was to the one he had set up for himself when he took the steamboat out of Portland to come home. He had not been weakened by his disaster. He was a bigger man than he had been before. The future stretching before him was infinitely better than he had imagined it could ever be.

"I love you too, Chance," she whispered. "And have ever since I had pigtails."

"You really got a hope chest?"

She tapped the rounded beauty of her breast. "In here. I never quit hoping."

"Me, neither," said Pace from the doorway. "But right now it's getting light, and we got a tussle coming."

Kitch and Ragan went out to the barn and took seat on a bale of hay. Through the archway, Ragan could see Pace on the front porch of the house, watching in the direction from which the riders would come again. Ragan did not think they would ride on to the house, instead returning to the point where they had lost track of him in the darkness. Pace could see when they showed up out there.

The light strengthened. Ragan was beginning to wonder if they were in for a long, tedious wait, or if his guess had been wrong, when he saw Pace stiffen in sudden attention. The rancher swung down off the porch at once and walked to the saddled horse he had kept waiting. He rose to leather and rode out.

"Get set," Kitch breathed.

Time seemed to hang suspended while they waited again. Finally Kitch murmured, "They're coming. Two or three of 'em."

Ragan also heard the beat of hoofs as horses came in fast, Then, all at once, a trio of riders whirled into the yard—Pace, Kildane, and Terrebine. There was grim satisfaction in the accuracy of his reasoning, but there was a dry, sour taste in Ragan's mouth.

Then a woman's voice rang out.

"Judd—Arch—it's a trap! Ragan and Dunsan are hiding in the—"

"Joy!" Kitch breathed. "And it sounds like Nancy clobbered her!"

Ragan was already moving, aware that now there would be

141

no dickering with those two men. Joy, in her seething search for a way to hit at him, had guessed more shrewdly than he had figured possible. He ran for the barn archway, fearing for Pace's safety. Terrebine had swung his horse and was bent on flight. Ragan's pistol cracked and the animal stumbled and came down. Terrebine threw himself onto its blind side and kept flattened. Pace, meanwhile had jerked up his sixgun. It swung to cover Kildane without a second to spare. Terrebine fired across the threshing body of the horse. Ragan heard the bullet whip past his head. He ran forward.

Seeing that his momentary fort was useless, Terrebine raised up. Two weapons seemed to fire in concert. Fear twisted the features of Terribine as he stared up on a slant at Ragan. There was no need to shoot again. Blood dribbled over his lower lip. Suddenly his head dropped. Ragan whirled to look at a white-faced Judd Kildane.

"On your own now, Judd," he said softly. "Younts is finished, too. Over on Fork." He stepped in, then, and took the pistol from the relaxed fingers of Arch Terrebine. He looked down for a long moment at his old partner, his more recent bitter enemy. The beating he had taken at Squabble Creek from this man was only a vague memory.

They ushered Judd into the house, where Nancy stood over a cowed Joy.

"How'd you shut her mouth for her?" Kitch asked, grinning at Nancy.

"I got there a little late," Nancy answered. "But with enough."

"Like to of seen it."

"Being a lady," said Nancy, "I'm glad you didn't."

Ragan produced the account book for what he hoped would be the last time. He didn't have to say a word to bring a shocked dismay to the faces of the two Kildanes. They stared at the book, then at Ragan, and finally at each other.

"And what's so temporary about that?" Nancy asked Joy.

"I—I don't even know what it is!" Joy stammered.

Judd flung her a look of bitter wrath. "No? Don't you try to shove the thing onto my shoulders, damn you!"

"So you had to keep books!" Joy blazed at him. "So you put it down in black and white! Well, it was your doing, the whole thing—and not mine!"

"The point," Ragan murmured, "is what you're going to do about it. Any smart man can take this book and prove what you've been up to. Nothing can change that now."

"What can I do?" Judd asked.

"It might go easier for you if you made amends."

"How."

"Pay for all that rustled beef."

"What with?"

"The proceeds."

Again rancor shaped the face of Judd as he swung his gaze to Joy. "All right," he rapped. "I'm going to serve time. You never had any love for me, and it'll give you all of Teeter. The gal who always straddled the fence, so she could climb off on the side that looked the most profitable. You played it smart from taw, Joy, but you fooled yourself."

Seeing the grim certainty on her brother's face, Joy widened her eyes.

"What do you mean?"

"Who'll pay for that beef? Arch and Angel are dead. The whole thing's been handled in cash. They never banked their share, they cached it. And who knows where to dig it up to pay their share of the bill?"

"That's your worry," Joy retorted.

"Is it? My profits weren't nearly big enough. It'd take a big chunk of Teeter to square up."

"Oh, no!" Joy cried, for the first time discerning what Judd meant, what the loss to her would be.

"Maybe that wasn't such a good fence you straddled," Nancy put in.

"You'll make amends, Judd?" Ragan asked.

"I won't get twenty years when there's a chance to get ten. Not to save her fine big ranch for her. Not to protect her precious position in this country."

"That lays the chunk," said Ragan. "Except the law will have some questions to ask Joy, too. Pace, you and Kitch want to escort them to the sheriff?"

Pace nodded, understanding his distaste for doing that himself. "Come on," he said to the Kildanes. "We're riding."

Ragan stared at the door through which the four of them vanished.

Then, with a long sigh, he said, "Well, I'm glad it's over."

"Oh, no," Nancy said, her eyes shining as she watched him. "We're glad that it's just beginning."

The End

Chad Merriman was the pseudonym Giff Cheshire used for his first novel, *Blood on the Sun*, published by Fawcett Gold Medal in 1952. He was born in 1905 on a homestead in Cheshire, Oregon. The county was named for his grandfather who had crossed the plains in 1852 by wagon from Tennessee, and the homestead was the same one his grandfather had claimed upon his arrival. Cheshire's early life was colored by the atmosphere of the Old West which in the first decade of the century had not yet been modified by the automobile. He attended public schools in Junction City and, following high school, enlisted in the U.S. Marine Corps and saw duty in Central America. In 1929 he came to the Portland area in Oregon and from 1929 to 1943 worked for the U.S. Corps of Engineers. By 1944, after moving to Beaverton, Oregon, he found he could make a living writing Western and North-Western short fiction for the magazine market, and presently stories under the byline Giff Cheshire began appearing in *Lariat Story Magazine*, *Dime Western*, and *North-West Romances*. His short story *Strangers in the Evening* won the Zane Grey Award in 1949. Cheshire's Western fiction was characterized from the beginning by a wider historical panorama of the frontier than just cattle ranching and frequently the settings for his later novels are in his native Oregon. *Thunder on the Mountain* (1960) focuses on Chief Joseph and the Nez Perce War, while *Wenatchee Bend* (1966) and *A Mighty Big River* (1967) are among his best-known titles. However, his Chad Merriman novels for Fawcett Gold Medal remain among his most popular works, notable for their complex characters, expert pacing, and authentic backgrounds.